I0713788

Millersburg Magick Mysteries #3

Magick and Murder

Suzan Harden

More books by Suzan Harden
(Each series is in suggested reading order)

Bloodlines

Blood Magick
Zombie Love
Zombie Confidential
Zombie Wedding
Amish, Vamps & Thieves
Blood Sacrifice
Love, War & a Bulldog
Zombie Goddess
Ravaged
Sacrificed
Reality Bites
Ghouls in the Grocery
Resurrected
Bloodlines Shorts Anthology
Bloodlines: The First Boxed Set

Justice

Sword and Sorceress 28 ("Justice")
Sword and Sorceress 30
("Diplomacy in the Dark")
Justice: The Beginning
A Question of Balance
A Modicum of Truth
A Matter of Death
A Touch of Mother
A Twist of Love
A Virtue of Child
A Hand of Father
A Measure of Knowledge
A Hint of Thief
A Cup of Conflict

The Justice Thalia Stories

Snowfall
Murder Most Fowl
The Sweetest Poison
A Granddaughter of Mine
Too Many Fish in the Sea

Tales of the Twelve

The Trickster Priestess and the Demon

Crossover Worlds

Invasion!

888-555-HERO

Hero De Facto
Hero Ad Hoc
Hero De Novo
A Very Hero Christmas
Hero De Jure
Hero In Camera
Hero Amicus Curiae
A Very Hero Wedding
A Very Hero New Year
Hero Ad Litem
Queer Eye for the Super Guy

Seasons of Magick

Spring
Summer
Autumn
Winter
The Seasons of Magick Anthology

Millersburg Magick Mysteries

Spells and Sleuths
Fae and Felonies
Magick and Murder

Soccer Moms of the Apocalypse

Pestilence in Pumpkin Spice
Famine in French Vanilla
War in White Chocolate
Death in Double Mocha
Demons Run at Halloween

Solar System Services, Inc.

Alone Is Not Lonely
Halloween Harvest ("A Place at the Table")

Miscellaneous

Sword and Sorceress 31 ("Pig-Headed")
Sword and Sorceress 32 ("Unexpected")
Practical Witches
Revenge Served Hot
The Yule Switch
Chocolate for Dinner
Silver Shoes and Pigs' Ears

For updates, news, and giveaways, join Suzan's mailing list or visit her website at suzanharden.com. You can also check her out on Facebook @SuzanHardenWriter.

suzanharden.blogspot.com/p/contact-me.html

This is a work of fiction. All characters, organizations and events in this story are products of the author's imagination and are not to be construed as real. Any resemblance to persons, living or dead, is entirely coincidental.

MAGICK AND MURDER
(Millersburg Magick Mysteries #3)

Copyright © 2024 by Suzan Harden
All rights reserved.

ISBN: 978-1-938745-80-5

Published by Angry Sheep Publishing
Findlay, Ohio

Interior Design by JW Manus
Cover Design by Valerie Lennox

*To owners and staff of the lamented Bake Shoppe
who made the greatest Long Johns ever*

Chapter 1 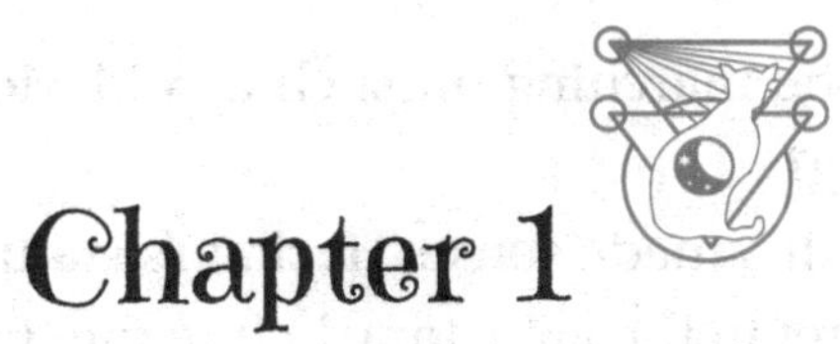

Kirsten Wilson kept an eye on the protesters across the street from Aunt Jo's coffee shop as she served their only two customers. The huge double-paned picture windows didn't block the crowd's shouts. The auras around the Normals who marched were ugly smears of gray, their hatred marring their usual rainbow colors. They paraded up and down the block of East Jackson Street in front of the Holmes County courthouse. The crowd shot even uglier looks at the coffee shop as they shouted their awful slogans.

She wished all of them were simply people from Cleveland or elsewhere, but she recognized more faces than she was comfortable with, including Hope Stillwell's mom and Josh Fairbanks and his mom. A shiver ran through Kirsten. She and Hope had been tight since first grade, and she'd been to the Stillwells for more birthdays and barbeques than she could count. To think Mrs. Stillwell harbored such a secret dislike for Kirsten made her sick.

At least, Josh had a plausible reason to march. In an attempt to start a race war between the fae and the other supernaturals, River Martin's mom had planted a mixed magick bomb on Josh. He'd been in the hospital for a week thanks to the effects of the energy leaking from the hodgepodge of charms Heather Martin had used.

People in Millersburg may get into a snit fit if the neighbor's dog pooped in their lawn or their cows trampled someone's garden. Maybe the occasional DUI or domestic abuse situation. But nothing so bigoted as marching in hatred because someone was different.

And she knew the crowd felt that hatred marrow deep. Why else would they be marching on such a cold Monday on the week of Thanksgiving?

None of this made sense. Heck, Jo's status as a witch had been an open secret in the area, long before the Rainier Outing revealed the existence of the supernatural races eleven years ago. The ladies in town often consulted her about their problems. A lot of farmers stopped in for a hot breakfast and even hotter coffee with a side helping of weather predictions. But with the current lawsuits questioning the supernaturals' status as United States citizens, some nasty elements in Normal society decided integration was something to be avoided at all costs.

An occasional dead leaf drifted down the street on the wind, a reminder the earth was settling in for her long winter sleep. But it was an unusually bright, sunny day for Ohio despite the steady, frigid breeze.

The brilliant blue sky silhouetted the historic three-story stone courthouse. However, its imposing features didn't deter the protesters. Neither did the couple of police officers watching them to make sure they didn't get out of hand. A couple of the idiots had tried to annoy people heading into the courthouse, both Amish and English alike. But after one warning from the police, Warren Simon, the leader of Humanity Now, reined in his followers.

Kirsten nibbled on her lower lip. Why did anyone follow a man like that? There was nothing really imposing about him. He was average height and average build for a Normal in his forties. His sandy brown hair was thinning on top. His round black spectacles gave him an owlish expression. Standard khaki slacks and a navy coat over his white shirt made him look like every other dad at the local basketball games. Scuffed dark brown loafers completed his middle-aged, fatherly ensemble. If he wasn't one of the top anti-supernatural leaders in the country, she would have mistaken him for an accountant.

Mary Levy joined Kirsten at the window. The ties of her prayer cap dangled over her shoulders, as startling white against her navy blue dress as her bleached apron. She'd given up on cleaning the tables, not that they really needed it. Her bucket of lemony sanitizer competed with the rich aroma of fresh ground beans. Beans that would go to waste. None of their usual weekday regulars were coming in. Not today. Not with the mob across the street.

"No good will come of this many angry English in town." Mary shook her head.

Even though Mary was a month younger than Kirsten, the Amish considered her an adult. Sometimes, Kirsten was envious of Mary's status in her religious community. Other times, not so much. Kirsten had been friends with Mary long before she met Hope, but the Levys never so much as commented on the Wilson family's differences from other English. Maybe because Mary's great-great-aunt had been a vampire.

The reporter from Cleveland's *The Plain Dealer* rose from his table. He'd come in for a sandwich and attempted to chat up Aunt Jo. She could be incredibly charming when she wanted to be, but she delivered only stiff politeness to him. The rest of the staff had followed her lead, maybe with a little less stiffness.

"Thank you, ladies." He nodded to Kirsten and Mary.

"Have a good day," Kirsten automatically replied with a smile.

He exited the café to a series of boos from the crowd that drowned out the ringing of the bell on the door. That left Rose Gleason, Jo's closest friend in town. The elderly, retired legal secretary sat in her usual seat in the front right corner of the café, sipping her cinnamon latte, and also watching the protesters across the street.

Jo joined Kirsten and Mary at the left window, her attention on the crowd as well. "Let's clean up and close up shop, ladies. We're not going to get much more business today."

"Isn't that giving in to these jerks?" Kirsten stared at her great-aunt. It wasn't like Jo to be intimidated by anyone.

You can protect yourself, Jo said silently. *Hell, even Rose can swing her cane like a pro polo player. But Mary won't defend herself if that crowd gets physical, and I don't want to see her hurt.*

She had a point.

Kirsten turned to Mary. "Let me give you a ride home."

For once, Mary didn't argue about being in a car. She merely nodded before she grabbed her bucket and continued wiping down the tables.

Twenty minutes later, everything had been swept, cleaned, and put away.

"Rose, I'll drop you off at your place," Jo said as the three of them put on their jackets. Mary placed her black bonnet on her head and wrapped her black shawl around her torso.

"I walked up here by myself," the seventy-year-old Normal snapped. "I can walk home." Rose strolled the six blocks from her old Victorian home to the coffee shop every day there wasn't rain, snow, or ice.

"Miz Rose," Mary said gently. "Not even I'm foolish enough to walk home with those people across the street. There's no sense courting trouble when it's avoidable."

Rose glared at the Amish girl overtop the bright orange rims of her spectacles. "Maybe a good whack over their heads would knock some sense into those idiots."

"That's assault and battery," Jo said. "And you know those assholes will press charges."

Rose's eyes narrowed behind her glasses. "What're you going to do? Hex me if I don't obey you?"

"Maybe I will, you old fart," Jo growled. Even though they were born the same year, Jo aged more slowly being a witch, which meant she could have passed for Kirsten's mom. Even her older sister.

Or maybe Rose's granddaughter.

Kirsten's leaned close to Mary and said not so quietly, "Is this what we're going to be like in fifty years?"

"Probably." Mary giggled. "But I will not be wearing such colorful eyewear—"

Glass exploded into the café from the right picture window.

And everyone in the café ducked.

# Chapter 2

Kirsten automatically shielded Mary and Rose with her body while Jo threw up a shield. Glass smacked the magickal ward and tinkled to the linoleum as the projectile cracked against wood. Jo muttered an obscenity and charged for the locked front doors.

"You two okay?" Kirsten asked her friends. Both women nodded. They all looked over at the chair that had been knocked over. A softball-sized river stone lay on the broken back slat of the chair. The same chair Rose had been sitting on a moment before. The projectile looked like the same stones the landscapers used as barriers around the flowering plants on the courthouse grounds.

Before Kirsten could reach her aunt, Jo had one of the doors unlocked and stormed outside. The bell jangled with her anger. Jeering and booing came from much closer, even accounting for the broken window. Kirsten raced after her. If Jo did anything to the crowd, it would only add ammunition to their claims that supernaturals were dangerous.

Outside, the protestors formed a semi-circle in the middle of the street, the open end facing Jo's Coffee Shop. Cars honked and a couple of truckers blared their horns, which added to the cacophony. The two officers assigned to keep an eye on the crowd tried to guide the members of Humanity Now back to the sidewalk in front of the courthouse, but they not only were ignored, but woefully outmatched.

Worse, Jo stood toe-to-toe with Warren Simon in the middle of the semi-circle. Kirsten couldn't catch exactly what they were shouting at each other between the honking and the crowd's shouts. Over the mob's heads, a familiar mahogany ponytail bounced toward them from South Monroe Street. Kirsten caught a mental whiff of Mom's fury.

"Rachel!" Cory Parsons, the *Monitor*'s staff photographer, towered over the crowd at six-six, and he jogged west on Jackson toward Mom's direction. She must have sent him out to snap some pictures of the protest, so he had to have seen the rock fly in the direction of Jo's coffee shop. Kirsten gave him props for trying to intercept Mom.

Rachel Wilson's job as the *Monitor*'s editor-in-chief was to report on events objectively. And neither Mom nor Jo were being very objective.

Kirsten ran out into the street and grabbed Jo's arm. "Come on, these jerks aren't worth it." She said the words aloud and telepathically so Mom would hear.

Jo jerked out of Kirsten's hold. "I'm going to sue your ass into the next century, Simon!"

"Go ahead!" he shouted back. "Then everyone will see your immorality!"

Kirsten pushed her body between Jo's and Simon's. *Don't let him bait you, Jo. He's doing this to make you look bad.*

"I don't care!" Jo jabbed her finger over Kirsten's shoulder. "They could have killed you or Mary or one of our customers!"

"And you breed heathen, Satan-loving sluts," Simon shouted behind Kirsten.

With the volatile emotion raging around them, someone really was going to get hurt. Where the heck had the two police officers disappeared to?

Jo, for the sake of the Goddess and everything on Earth, please go inside!

A troubled look appeared on Jo's face. Maybe their predicament was finally getting through to her. She took a hesitant step back, obviously forced herself to calm down, and took two more steps back.

Kirsten relaxed a hair and started to follow Jo when someone plowed into her from behind.

She'd been body-checked on the court enough times over the years of playing basketball. Fighting the instinct to put her arms out, she curled and rolled with the force of the shove.

Except the asphalt of Jackson Street was a heck of a lot harder than the wooden boards that formed the floor of the West Holmes High School gymnasium. The landing knocked every molecule of air out of her lungs.

The crowd surged forward. Primal fear consumed her. This crowd wanted blood. Her blood.

A fireball whizzed over her head between her and the throng. It exploded short of the protestors, but the display of magick startled the Humanity Now mob into silence. The acrid odor of human fear permeated the street.

"Get the hell away from my daughter!"

Mom.

The one person who never displayed her talents in public.

Chapter 3 

Kirsten scrambled to her feet. Mom and Jo stood side-by-side. Fireballs glowed in their hands. The crowd murmured, their hate and fear evident, but none of them dared to take a step forward.

"You dare to threaten us in front of officers of the law?" Simon sneered.

"You assaulted a citizen of Millersburg." Police Chief Patricia Hall marched toward the standoff.

She wasn't alone. Three more officers followed her. In the distance, sirens wailed. The chief must have called the sheriff's department for backup. She stopped beside Kirsten.

"Are you all right, Ms. Wilson?" Chief Hall eyed her with a bit of worry as she held out a hand to help up Kirsten.

She took the chief's hand, stood, and rubbed her diaphragm to get the kink out that was making it difficult to breathe properly. "I had worse from a Tri-Valley player during last year's regional tournament." It hurt to take more than a shallow sip of air, but she was pretty sure nothing was broken.

"Would you like to press charges?"

"She's a child," one of the women in the crowd shouted.

"I'm not the one dumb enough to assault a child in front of five law officers," Chief Hall replied mildly. "Or her mother."

"She tried to kill us." Simon jabbed his right index finger in the direction of Mom. Several of his cronies nodded and muttered in agreement.

"If I wanted to kill you, we wouldn't be having this conversation," Mom said calmly.

"I want to file charges," Jo spat. "Take a look at what these asshats did to my shop. One of them threw a stone through my window. They're damn lucky they didn't hurt anyone."

Chief Hall eyed the window and turned back to the crowd. "One of you want to take responsibility, or shall I charge every protestor with disorderly conduct?"

"We have a right to defend ourselves," Simon shouted.

"You don't have a right to vandalize property and tie up downtown traffic," Chief Hall said. Someone in the direction of South Mason Street honked their car horn as if to emphasize the police chief's point.

"You can't violate our first amendment rights!" Simon shouted. From the news clips Kirsten had seen, that seemed to be his method of choice for dealing with things when he knew he was losing.

She counted to twenty before the chief smiled and sweetly said, "If that's the way you want to play it, Mr. Simon." She raised her voice. "Officers, every protest participant gets a ticket if they don't get back on the sidewalk in ten seconds. Ten, nine, eight . . ."

Most of the protestors scrambled back to the sidewalk in front of the courthouse, everyone except for Simon and a couple of others.

"Seven, six, five . . ." Chief Hall continued. Kirsten held her breath.

"Warren, don't," A dark-haired woman pleaded. "It's not worth making these snowflakes look like the good guys."

"Get on the sidewalk, Vicki," Simon said over his shoulder. Even as this Vicki and the last of his followers retreated, he stood toe-to-toe with Mom. "You are going to hell."

Mom clenched her fists and extinguished her fireballs. "As a member of the press, I also have certain first amendment rights. You'd better remember that."

Her statement broke Cory's paralysis at the confrontation. He started snapping more pictures. Kirsten couldn't blame the guy for freezing at the confrontation in the middle of Jackson Street. The most excitement in town was usually high school games, car accidents, and the occasional fire.

"Two, one." Chief Hall reached for her handcuffs on her utility belt. "Warren Simon, you are under arrest for disorderly conduct. You have the right to remain silent—"

The rest of her recitation of the Miranda warning was swallowed by a chorus of boos and jeers from the protestors. Sheriffs' deputies joined the police officers to form a wall between the crowd and the street. Eastbound traffic started to ease down Jackson Street while Chief Hall cuffed Simon.

Jo extinguished her fireballs as well, pivoted on her heel and marched back to her café. However, Mom and Simon continued to glare at each other.

Kirsten grabbed Mom's arm and tugged on her. "Come on. Let's get out of the street before Chief Hall has to arrest us, too."

"Yes, run while you can, witch," Simon spat.

Mom stepped closer to him. "I'd be very careful about who I threaten if I were you."

"Rachel, step back," Chief Hall barked.

"C'mon, Mom." The last thing Kirsten wanted was to fight publicly with her own mother, but better that than getting into a brawl with the police or the protesters. No one would look good in that situation.

Mom relented, and the two of them retreated to the café. Kirsten glanced over her shoulder. Chief Hall escorted Simon to a squad car, but she stopped and exchanged words with Sheriff Birkheimer.

Inside the coffee shop, Jo took pictures of the damage to her store with her cell phone while Kirsten settled Mom in a chair on the other side of the dining area. Mary hurried back to the cooler and retrieved a bottle of water. She brought it over to Mom who accepted it with a tired smile.

"Thank you, Mary," Mom murmured. All the tension flowed out

of her, but she gripped Kirsten's hand tightly. "I'm glad you kept your head out there, honey, but you shouldn't have confronted those idiots."

"Me confront them?" Kirsten squeezed Mom's hand. "I seem to recall it was you and Jo tossing threats and fireballs. Besides, I was only trying to get Jo back inside before she did something stupid."

"Me do something stupid?" Jo lowered her phone. "I didn't start throwing rocks!"

The bell hanging on the door rang. Everyone jumped. Sheriff Birkheimer poked his head around the edge. To Kirsten and her twin sister Kaley, he would always be Uncle Jimmy, their godfather, but he was obviously here in his official capacity.

"Can I come in, ladies?"

"That depends," Jo folded her arms over her chest. "What are you planning to do?"

"Now, Jo, you know I'm not your enemy." He removed his hat and ran his hand over his short brown hair. "I'm here to make sure you guys are all right, and take your statements regarding the broken window."

He replaced his hat and pulled out his notebook and pen from his pocket. For the next half hour, he asked questions of the four people who had been in the coffee shop when the rock crashed through the window. Another deputy came in and took pictures. Jo's phone rang, and she disappeared back in her office, probably to discuss the damages with her insurance company.

"Why are you really keeping us here, Jimmy?" Mom adopted the same cross-armed, wide-feet posture Jo had when he came in.

"You, of all people, know a reporter shouldn't be part of the story, Rachel." His tone was calm, but there was something in his eyes.

"Warren Simon wants you to file charges against Mom, doesn't he?" Kirsten said.

"His lawyer has already called the mayor and the county commissioners." Jimmy was obviously not happy about the situation from the way he fidgeted. "If we file charges against him, it'll be all over the national news that we didn't hold a witch to the same standards as a Normal."

Mom jabbed her left index finger in Kirsten's direction. "They threatened my daughter!"

"But they didn't throw a fireball at her." He tapped his pen against his notebook pad.

"No, they threw a stone through my aunt's shop window!" The unfairness of the entire situation galled Kirsten, even though she knew how this would end.

"Did any of you get pictures or video of the jerk who threw it?" Jimmy asked.

Kirsten sagged. Mom, Mary, and Rose all shook their heads.

"They've got video of Mom throwing the fireball, don't they?" Kirsten hugged herself.

"Yeah." Jimmy grimaced. "Damn thing's already been uploaded to the Humanity Now website and getting hits. It doesn't make you look good, Rachel."

Mom muttered a two-word phrase Kirsten had never heard her say, but it definitely applied to the protesters. Mary covered her mouth with both hands over the obscenity, her eyes wide.

"Tell Jo I'll swing by with the incident report when I get my coffee in the morning. Try to keep your nose clean, Rachel." He tucked his notebook and pen back in his inside coat pocket. "Same goes for you, too, Kirsten. Neither Pat or I want you to lose that law enforcement internship for next year." He nodded to everyone before he stalked out of the café, the deputy with the camera on his heels.

"What do we do about the window?" Mary asked.

"We clean up the glass and see if we can get a delivery from the lumberyard in the next hour," Kirsten said. She headed for the back room of the store to fetch the broom, the dustpan, and the huge heavy-duty rubber trash can.

Simon had definitely been trying to goad Jo into doing something stupid. Unfortunately, Mom delivered what the Humanity Now idiots wanted. Now, they knew why, but what on earth did they do to stop the organization from using that blasted video against all supernaturals?

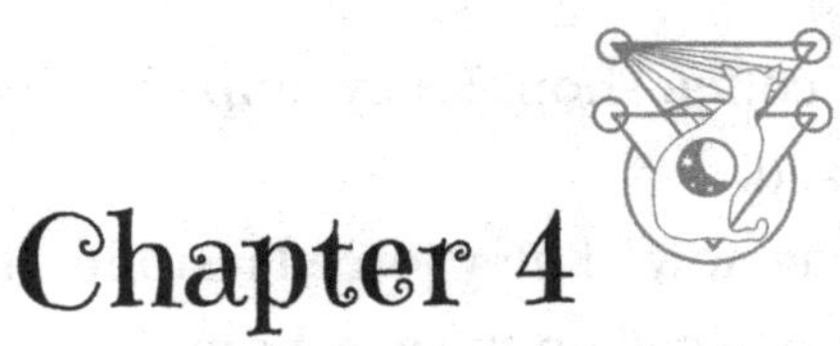

Chapter 4

Standing in the canned fruits and vegetables aisle at the IGA, Kaley checked her list again and made a face. "Now where the heck is the cranberry sauce?"

"End cap." River Martin pointed to the other end of the aisle. "All the canned pumpkin is down there, too."

It was kind of weird shopping with him like they were a couple. Which they weren't. At least, not officially though Donny Fryer and Mandy Jenkins teased her about it. River had asked to take things slow when it came to their joint attraction. Kaley couldn't blame him. A new town and a new school was bad enough without all the crap that came with him being half-fae.

She consulted the list. "Then, we need green beans, fried onions, and mushrooms."

"Whole, cut, or French-style?" he asked as he stared at the shelves in front of him.

"Whole. Six cans." She grabbed two canisters of the crunchy fried onions, but pain jabbed her right side. She couldn't catch her breath, and she dropped the canisters into the cart instead of setting them gently on the heavy steel wires.

River grabbed her as she started to go down. *What's wrong?*

Something's happened to Kirsten. Kaley took tiny sips of air. *The last time I felt something like this, a Tri-Valley player tripped her during a tournament game last year, and the fall knocked the wind out of her.*

And now? River's eyes shifted from light blue to storm gray.

Kaley wasn't about to mention the surge of fear from her twin. Whatever had happened was over. Kirsten could have slipped and fallen at the coffee shop. Kaley gulped a deep breath as her diaphragm relaxed.

"She's okay now." Kaley forced a smile. "Let's finish up in here, and I'll give her a call on the way home."

"You sure?" River's magick grated and buzzed along Kaley's nerves, but the focus was his worry about her.

She nodded. "I'm sure."

He released her and turned back to the shelves. "About the mushrooms, pieces or slices?"

"Slices. Two small cans or one large."

River paused with the large can in his hand. "What do these go in?"

"The green bean casserole, silly."

He frowned. "No one I know puts mushrooms in their green bean casserole."

"They use cream of mushroom soup, don't they?"

"Yeah, but . . ."

"What's the problem? Your dad's people dance around mushroom patches. That's the reason they're called fairy circles." She waved her hand nonchalantly in a desperate effort to act as she usually did. Once she was over the shock of Kirsten's pain, Mom's anger and worry filtered through her mind.

River shook his head and made a face at her. "That's so racist."

Kaley cocked her head while she tried to focus on him. "What? How?"

"Do you make jokes about Donny Fryer peeing on hydrants? Do you make cracks about Carmen Alonzo driving a taco truck?"

"Oh." Kaley winced. "I didn't think about it that way. I'm really sorry." Crap, she'd definitely screwed up. Maybe she wasn't as free of prejudice as she thought.

"Not to mention fairy is right up there with the n-word." River made a slashing motion with his hand. "That's a good way to find yourself at the pointy end of a sword."

"The pointy end of a sword?" She grinned.

Red flooded his face and ears at her deliberate double entendre. His ears were decidedly round like his Normal mom's were.

"You know what I mean," he said.

"Do tell." She giggled.

River ignored her comment. He grabbed a couple cans of pumpkin and cranberry sauce and place them in their cart before he tugged on the basket end. "What's next on the list?"

"Nice try in changing the subject." But she consulted her list. "We also need raisins for the mincemeat pie."

River made a face. "Mincemeat?"

Kaley rolled her eyes as they turned the corner and walked down the next aisle to where the dried fruit was located. "Dad loves it, and Mom made a point of asking Grandma Wilson for the recipe because it's his favorite. Personally, I'm not a big fan of meaty and sweetie in the same dish."

"So, no pineapple with your ham?" He grabbed a bag of the store-brand raisins.

"That's the one exception, and it's got to be on pizza," she muttered.

Her phone buzzed, and she pulled the device out of her jeans pocket. A sick feeling ran through her as she read Kirsten's message. Her sister's fall hadn't been an accident.

A ton of curse words raced through Kaley's mind. She whirled around, examining each shopper's face in the aisle. Where would the next threat come from?

"Hey." River grabbed her arm. "What happened?"

She couldn't say a word past the lump of fear in her throat. She'd never been afraid of people in her hometown.

Not before today.

River gently cupped her right hand and raised it so he could see her phone screen. His eyes narrowed, and his lips thinned.

"Let's get your mom's groceries," he said softly. "That'll be one thing off her mind. And Grandma and I will definitely be at your house on Thursday."

Kaley swallowed hard and nodded. "She's bringing the sweet potatoes, right?"

He grinned. "With lots of marshmallow fluff."

"Fluff? Not mini-marshmallows?"

"Trust me, you like this better. She used me to test her recipe. More marshmallow to potato flavor."

"All right." She nodded again.

River released her hand, and she found herself missing his touch. She shoved her phone back in her front jeans pocket and snatched up Mom's list to cover her discomfiture. "Let's grab the flour and salt before heading to the dairy section."

They raced as quickly as they could around the other shoppers and collected the remaining items on Mom's grocery list. Except when they reached the check-out lanes, every register had a line, and the other shoppers stared at her. However, it wasn't the usual friendly faces of people recognizing one of the high school cheerleaders from her letterman jacket.

The elderly woman in line in front of Kaley gave her an odd look before she crossed herself. Now, what was that all about? Kaley frowned. It wasn't like she was wearing pentacles, and there was no way the woman could know about her steel triquetra key chain. The elderly woman slammed the divider down after her items and glared at Kaley as if daring her to move it.

She swallowed her unease. They just needed to get the groceries rung up and paid for so they could get the heck out of the store. She and River unloaded items in the cart onto the conveyor belt.

Thankfully, they were in Shannon Murphy's lane. Shannon had

been Kaley and Kirsten's babysitter when they were little. Her husband passed away shortly after he retired, and she started working at the grocery store, more to do something than to supplement her savings.

"Hey, Shannon."

"Hey, kiddo!" Shannon's wide smile helped ease the tension in Kaley's shoulders. "Your mom gotcha doing the Thanksgiving shopping, huh?"

"Yeah, she's doing things up big since she's afraid Kirsten and I will never come home for a holiday again once we head off to college." Kaley grabbed her stack of reusable bags and started sacking groceries.

"And your friend?" Shannon said coyly.

"River, this is our former nanny Shannon." Kaley chuckled at her old babysitter's antics. "River is Cissy Martin's grandson."

"I'd heard Heather and her boy had moved back here. Nice to meet you, River." Shannon nodded to him.

At least, she had the grace not to mention River's mom currently resided in a psychiatric hospital after the county judge deemed her mentally unfit to stand trial. It had been a rough month for River because of his mom's criminally insane actions.

"Ma'am." He moved to the end of the line and started putting the cold items into the insulated bag.

"Kaley Wilson!"

Goddess, what now? She steeled herself at the familiar voice before she turned to face Mrs. Ryder, the mother of the captain of the West Holmes cheerleading squad. "Yes, ma'am?"

"Your mother is just as dangerous as you are!" Mrs. Ryder shrieked as she waved her phone in Kaley's face.

"What?" Kaley couldn't make out anything on the video playing on the phone with Mrs. Ryder's jerky motions.

River inserted himself in front of Mrs. Ryder and grabbed her wrist in mid-swing. "Watch what you're doing."

"Let me go," she spat.

"Then quit trying to hit Kaley," he bit back. When Mrs. Ryder tried to jerk out of his grip, he let her go. She stumbled, but caught herself before she landed on the floor.

"What's going on here?" The store manager Mr. Bickle strode toward Shannon's aisle, a distraught expression on his face.

"Why are you allowing those people to shop in your store?" Mrs. Ryder screeched.

"What people?" Mr. Bickle looked thoroughly confused.

"That bitch put a hex on my daughter!" Mrs. Ryder pointed at Kaley.

"Your daughter tried to hit me, and I ducked," Kaley protested. "It's not my fault she's a clumsy cow and screwed up her knee."

"Ladies, please." Mr. Bickle looked like he was about to cry behind his wire rims.

"Of course, you get it straight from your mother!" Mrs. Ryder shook her phone at Kaley.

Shannon waddled from behind her register. "Do we need to call the police, or are you going to leave quietly, Sandra?"

"You're going to let that little bitch stay?" Mrs. Ryder's shock that someone took Kaley's side was mirrored by a few other people. Everyone else simply appeared disgusted.

Shannon crossed her arms and glared at Mrs. Ryder. "That little girl ain't the one causing a scene in public. You are. Now, once again, do I need to call the police or are you going to leave peaceably?"

Realizing Shannon was the proverbial immoveable object, Mrs. Ryder turned to Mr. Bickle. "Are you going to let your employee insult me like that?"

The manager seemed to find his backbone. He straightened

and glared at Mrs. Ryder. "The only one tossing out insults and creating a disturbance here is you."

"I'm going to report you to the owner," Mrs. Ryder said.

Shannon pointed overhead. "Make sure you tell him about the security video capturing your performance when you call him. Oh, wait. Isn't Ron Schneider your ex-husband?"

Mrs. Ryder blinked rapidly, shocked by the turnaround in circumstances. More than half of the crowd watching the drama tittered. Seeing no allies, she pivoted and marched out of the grocery store.

Shannon waddled back to her register. Kaley tried to breathe normally as she slipped Mom's debit card into the reader. It took a couple of tries to get the PIN right. She could feel all the eyes in the store on her. Finally, the device beeped, and she pulled out the card.

River had bagged the rest of the groceries and loaded them into the cart.

Shannon handed Kaley the receipt and gave her a reassuring smile. "You tell your mom and dad hello for me."

"I will." Kaley waved. "Happy Thanksgiving."

"You too, darling."

Kaley and River headed for the exit. She sagged when she saw Mrs. Ryder still in the parking lot. Amelia's mom was speaking with a man Kaley didn't recognize.

He was a few inches taller than Mrs. Rider. He wore a brown leather jacket and jeans. His dark hair was just long enough not to be a buzz cut, but too short to be a crew cut. But the most prominent feature was a jagged scar down his cheek. The pair looked toward Kaley and River with ugly expressions on their faces.

Kaley and River quickly loaded their bags into the back of his ancient blue Jeep. Mrs. Ryder and the gentleman with her were still staring at them.

"Take a selfie," River whispered.

"What?"

He wrapped an arm around her waist and held her so their backs were to Mrs. Ryder and the stranger. Her body immediately warmed at his touch, but she did as he asked and took a picture of Amelia's mom and the stranger.

"Can you do a close-up of the guy with Mrs. Ryder?" River whispered.

Kirsten swallowed and changed the settings. River nodded when he saw the resulting photo. "Send a copy to me."

"Why?"

"In case anything happens to your phone. Get in the car," River whispered. "I'll take care of the cart."

"Don't do anything stupid," Kaley whispered back.

"Who? Me?" River shot her a devilish grin.

That expression sent a shiver through her. No wonder Olivia Burke looked at him like a prime Angus steak. And Olivia wasn't into guys. If he was anything like his sidhe relatives, Kaley could see why River's mom had fallen under his dad's spell. She nodded and climbed into the passenger seat of River's Jeep.

It never failed to amaze her how clean the interior of his Jeep was compared to the vehicles of all the other guys in school. And it always smelled like cedar and baklava inside though he didn't have an air freshener anywhere. She had checked.

Fae magick jabbed Kaley's psyche, and despite feeling the need to raise a ward, she concentrated to keep her own power from reacting to the alien sensation. River opened the driver side door and slid into the seat. A self-satisfied smirk tilted his mouth.

She crossed her arms. "What did you do?"

"Nothing that'll harm anyone."

"What. Did. You. Do."

"You're not the only one who has talent with air." He grinned and backed out of their parking space.

As they drove past Mrs. Ryder, Kaley could see the tires on her Cadillac. Especially the flat front left tire.

While she didn't blame River, his stunt was going to come back to bite them in the ass. Especially with the Humanity Now protesters in town.

Chapter 5

Kirsten glanced at Mary as she drove toward the Levy farm. "Look, I know how much you dislike me giving you a ride, but you'd better let me pick you up for work in the morning."

Mary nodded curtly. "Yes, that may be best. However, I may have another ride."

"Another ride?"

"Aunt Anne and Uncle Colin are coming to visit," Mary said. "They are in Philadelphia right now with his family, but they should be here sometime tomorrow."

Kirsten tried to quell the sudden pounding of her heart. Both of Mary's relatives had been vampires before the cure for the V-virus was developed when Kirsten and Kaley were in first grade. Colin and Anne usually stopped by to see Mom and Jo when they were in town.

"If you have family coming in, why didn't you take the rest of the week off when Jo offered?" Kirsten asked.

"Because my reason is vain," Mary whispered.

"Vain?" Kirsten couldn't imagine her friend remotely having an ego much less allowing it to control her.

"Yes." Mary cleared her throat. "Elijah Miller has asked Father and Joshua's permission to court me." Except she didn't sound too sure about the situation.

"I thought you had a thing for Elijah." Kirsten hit the turn signal for the township road and pressed the brake pedal.

"I do, as he does for me."

Kirsten completed the turn and glanced at Mary again. She blushed like she did every time Elijah's name was mentioned.

"And?"

"Uncle Joseph had written to Father that the farm next to his in Kentucky was for sale." Mary played with the ends of her shawl. "He thought one of my brothers might be interested. However, Father sent the payment to Uncle Joseph and told Elijah the farm would be ours."

"And you're saving your money to pay for the rest?"

"No, to pay Father back." Mary shook her head. "A farm is too much for a wedding gift."

This time Kirsten's heart pounded for a different reason. "What you're really saying is you're leaving Holmes County?"

"Yes," Mary said. "But not until after our wedding next spring."

"You're seventeen. He's nineteen. Why wait to get married if you have your parents' permission?" Kirsten shrugged though a part of her heart was breaking. After all her talk of leaving Millersburg, Mary would leave first? It definitely was not how she'd envisioned things.

"He will be finished with his carpenter apprenticeship in March," Mary firmly stated. "In the meantime, I will continue my work with Jo to earn the money for our own farm."

"You know, I think I'm a little jealous of you," Kirsten murmured.

"Jealous of me?"

"Moving on with your life." Kirsten flipped the turn signal for the driveway into the Levys' farm. Or one of the farms anyway. Mary's brother Joshua had inherited this one from their great-grandfather Thomas. Mary had moved in with them when she was ten to help when Joshua's wife had a very difficult first pregnancy.

"But you will be going to college in less than two years," Mary protested.

"I mean getting out of Millersburg." Kirsten frowned. A silver SUV was parked by the barn next to the Levys' buggy. "It looks like you guys have visitors."

"Perhaps Aunt Anne has come early." Mary's face lit up like it was Santa's sleigh sitting there. "You must come in and say hello."

A pack of border collies rushed Mom's sedan as Kirsten braked next to the house. The dogs were followed by a gaggle of children, both Amish and English.

Mary jumped out of the car and hugged all the kids. Kirsten couldn't help smiling at them as they talked excitedly over each other while she climbed out of the car. She bent over and greeted the five dogs tumbling over each other to get the most pets.

At the sound of the back door, Kirsten looked up. Colin Fitzgerald strode out of the farmhouse. Silver decorated his auburn hair now that he was aging again. He wore jeans and a Princeton sweatshirt.

"Hey, ladies!" He hugged Mary while five of the six kids swarmed over Kirsten.

"Oh, my goddess! You guys have gotten so big!" she said as she gave all of them hugs.

The littlest girl in a navy jacket stood a few feet away and nibbled on her index finger. She couldn't have been more than three, and she definitely had Colin's hair color.

"It's okay, Sammi," Patrick said. The eight-year-old was Colin and Anne's eldest child. "Kirsten's a witch." That was an interesting introduction.

Kirsten knelt to be closer to the little girl's eye-level. "I know you don't remember me, Sammi. You were a baby the last time I saw you."

"I'm not a baby now," the little girl said fiercely.

"No, you're definitely not." Kirsten smiled.

"If you're a witch, prove it." Sammi crossed her arms and scowled at Kirsten.

"Samantha Ruth Fitzgerald!" An appalled expression crossed Colin's face.

"No problem." Kirsten concentrated on the pile of red maple leaves on top of the mulch bed near the sleeping garden. She lifted one leaf and danced it along the breeze she created. Air was a little harder to work with than water, but she wasn't about to soak the crowd of children and dogs with the cold weather. "Hold your hand out, Sammi." The little girl complied with Kirsten's request, and she landed the leaf on Sammi's upraised palm.

Sammi twisted her little mouth. "I s'pose that'll do."

"Thank you." Kirsten resisted the urge to grin as she rose.

Naomi, Joshua's eldest daughter, tugged on Kirsten's hand. "Come in and see Aunt Anne!"

Laughing, Kirsten followed the kids into the house. She couldn't help but notice Sammi clung to the red leaf as she trooped inside the farmhouse with the rest of the children. Colin's wife Anne stood by the pump sink and peeled potatoes.

Another girl Kirsten didn't recognize violently punched bread dough on a floured section of the wooden counter. Her blue-black hair, brilliant blue eyes, and super pale skin were a major contrast to the coloring of either the Levy or Fitzgerald clans.

Mary's sister-in-law Dinah looked up from the oven. "What are you doing home so early? Kirsten?"

"Sorry to interrupt your family time." Kirsten waggled her fingers.

"It's all right." Dinah smiled as she closed the oven door and wiped her hands on her apron. "Would you like to stay for supper?"

"No, thank you." Kirsten hated asking, but talking to an actual enforcer would be a good idea, given the incident in front of Jo's coffee shop. "Um, Miz Anne, could I talk to you privately?"

The former vampire had been roughly Kirsten's age when she was Turned. Technically, her physical age was now twenty-nine, but in reality, she was nearly one hundred. She frowned but nodded and wiped her hands on a kitchen towel. "Let me get my coat."

"Naomi, you want to finish beating up this dough for me," the girl at the counter said.

"Eleanor, we do not use violent language in this house." Dinah frowned at the girl.

"Sorry, Dinah." But she didn't sound that sorry.

"Kirsten, that's Ellie," Colin said. "Ellie, Kirsten."

"Kirsten's a witch," Sammi said. "She gave me this." The little girl held up her leaf.

"Awesome." No longer looking bored, Ellie grinned at Kirsten.

Which was a little weird. This Ellie was obviously Normal from her aura, but since she didn't blink at Sammi's announcement, she was probably Family.

Family no longer had the connotation it used to, but a lot of the older supernatural folks still clung to the term. It used to mean a Normal related by blood or marriage who could be trusted with the knowledge of the supernatural.

Now days, it simply meant a trusted Normal.

Ellie and Anne grabbed their jackets and followed Kirsten, Colin, and Mary out onto the back porch. Dinah wrangled the little kids back into the kitchen when they attempted to follow the older people outside.

Mary's brother Joshua was climbing the steps to the porch when they all exited. "Kirsten, a pleasure to see you, but what's going on?"

"The Humanity Now protesters harassed customers at the coffee shop," Mary said. "One of them threw a stone through one of the shop's front windows, but we did not see who did it. They then tried to goad Jo into attacking them when she confronted them about the damage. When that did not work, they pushed Kirsten to the pavement and threatened additional violence against her."

"And Mom threw a fireball to get them away from me," Kirsten added.

"Rachel?" Colin stared at Kirsten in disbelief. "Threw a fireball in public?"

"Yeah." She turned to Miz Anne. "That's why I wanted to speak with you. We don't have any enforcers in Millersburg, and I'd like some advice."

"You have an enforcer now." Ellie crossed her arms and scowled.

Miz Anne ignored the girl and sat on the porch swing. "I thought Julia Wolford moved back here and had become a sheriff's deputy."

Kirsten nodded. "She has, but she's technically not an enforcer like her dad. Sheriff Birkheimer and Police Chief Hall are putting together a joint task force to deal with supernatural problems, and they've asked me to intern when basketball season's over next spring. However, that may be too late."

"Why haven't you contacted the chief enforcer of Brown Dog?" Miz Anne asked.

"Because she'll just give Mom and Jo the same grief about moving back to Cleveland." Kirsten shoved her hands in her coat pockets. "If supernaturals are going to prove we've integrated into society, we can't keep running to our leaders every time something goes wrong."

"Wow." Ellie rolled her eyes. "Where have we heard that speech before?"

"What did the police do after Rachel threw the fireball?" Joshua said.

"They cuffed Warren Simon when he deliberately refused to obey their orders about not blocking traffic on Jackson." Kirsten leaned against the porch railing. "He wants charges pressed against Mom for assault."

"Given the circumstances, it sounds like a case of self-defense," Colin said.

Joshua eyed his sister. "Maybe it would be best for you to stay here tomorrow."

"No!" Mary's expression was fiercer than Sammi's had been earlier. "I will not abandon my friends!"

"Putting yourself at risk isn't worth paying your dad back," Kirsten said.

Mary blushed under the rays of the setting sun that filtered through the scudding clouds.

"The money that purchased the farm in Kentucky wasn't a loan, Mary," Anne said softly. "And it wasn't only from your father. It is a wedding present. Everyone in the family contributed, including Colin and me."

"But-but—" The moisture in Mary's eyes gleamed.

"It's a present," Colin reiterated. "You are not paying any of us back for a wedding gift."

She swiped at her face with the back of her hand. "I still won't abandon my friends in their difficulty."

"What if I go to the café with Kirsten and Mary in the morning?" Ellie said. "Jo will have a trained enforcer on site—"

"And you have your aunt's tendency to find trouble." Colin wore a wry smile.

"Thank you for not comparing me to my mother, Uncle Colin." Ellie grinned.

That explained why this Ellie accompanied the Fitzgerald family to Ohio. Both Colin and Anne still worked for the St. James Vampire Coven even though they'd taken the cure for the V-virus. Master St. James would never allow two trusted lieutenants, especially if they were Normal, to go into another vampire's territory without some type of protection.

Though Master St. James was a god now, not a vampire or a Normal, thanks to his wife.

"I should go instead," Anne said.

"But—" Ellie protested.

"As you said, it would be a good idea to have an *experienced* enforcer on site." Anne gave her a look that brooked no argument.

"Actually, Ellie might be a better idea." Kirsten quivered when everyone looked at her. "My sister's boyfriend who's half-fae and another friend of ours who's a werecoyote have volunteered to hang out at the store, plus the entire West Holmes girls' basketball team. Ellie would fit in better." She turned to the enforcer. "If you're willing to work with us."

"C'mon, Anne," Ellie said. "You're here to visit with your family. Let me check things out. If there's real trouble, we can call Dare and Brown Dog Covens."

Miz Anne made a displeased face.

"C'mon, honey, you know Jimmy's not going to object to some extra help," Colin said.

"I don't know anything about this Chief Hall," Anne protested.

"She's of the same mind as Sheriff Birkheimer," Joshua said. "Tolerant of all as long as the citizens of Millersburg behave themselves."

"All right." Miz Anne raised her hands in surrender. "I guess I should have known Ellie would be bored here on the farm."

"It's not a question of boredom," Ellie shot back. "It's a question of people being threatened when they've done nothing wrong. At least, that's what my coven enforcement trainer kept harping about."

"I don't appreciate my words being thrown back in my face." Miz Anne frowned at the girl.

"It's settled." Kirsten pushed off the railing. "I'll swing by at four-thirty in the morning to pick up you guys."

"Four-thirty?" Ellie stared at her. "In the morning?"

Joshua and Mary laughed.

Kirsten shrugged. "Folks start early around here."

"During Thanksgiving Break, too?" Ellie looked totally appalled.

"Yep." Kirsten grinned.

"I'm still on Los Angeles time." Ellie flopped onto the porch swing next to Miz Anne.

"If you will be too tired—" Anne started.

"Never mind." Ellie held up her hands. "I'll take a nap before it's time to leave." She looked up at Kirsten. "Please tell me you have an espresso machine at this café of yours."

"I even know how to make a mean mocha." Kirsten smiled.

"I think you and I are going to be besties." Ellie grinned back.

Chapter 6

Kaley stirred the vegetables in their largest frying pan while Kirsten dealt with the fettucine and alfredo sauce. Uncle Jimmy and Dad sat on stools on the other side of the breakfast counter and discussed the confrontation with Humanity Now this afternoon.

"Patty couldn't keep that Simon fella longer than it took to process him." Jimmy took a swig of his root beer. Dad had offered him a real beer, but the sheriff was technically on duty, and this was his dinner break.

"But he threatened my family—" Dad began.

"Simon didn't actually do anything, Ethan. Rach did." Sheriff Birkheimer sighed. "Speaking of which, Kaley, you want to give me your version of what happened at the IGA."

She gulped. "How did you find out? Did Mr. Bickle call you?"

"No, I got an earful from Shannon Murphy on the phone this afternoon," he said.

"Kaley, what the hell is Jimmy talking about?" Dad cocked his head.

"Hey, the broccoli's burning!" Kirsten nudged Kaley aside and turned off the gas to the front right burner.

"Sorry," Kaley murmured.

"I'll finish dinner," Kirsten said and followed with an apologetic smile. "You need to tell Jimmy what happened."

Kaley stepped across the kitchen and leaned her elbows on the breakfast counter. She spilled everything that had happened from Kirsten's text about the trouble at Jo's coffee shop to the man Mrs. Ryder was speaking with in the grocery store parking lot.

Well, everything except for River's stunt with the flat tire on Mrs. Ryder's car.

When she finished, Jimmy rubbed his chin. "Well, that pretty much matches what Shannon said up to you and the Martin boy leaving the store."

"Amelia and her parents have been the proverbial thorn in my side since I started gymnastics and dance in grade school, but that's normal female rivalry." Kaley shook her head. "The racist crap Mrs. Ryder spewed is new."

"Well, frankly, none of you Wilson gals made a public spectacle until this fall between the ghost dog and the bombings," Sheriff Birkheimer said. "Rumors are one thing. Eyewitnesses are another. Seeing what Jo and the three of you are actually capable of has changed a lot of people's minds. With that case going to the Supreme Court this term, folks are getting riled up."

"This is ridiculous," Dad snapped. "I grew up here. Rach and I have lived in this town ever since we graduated from college. The only thing that's changed is their actual knowledge of Jo and Rach's background."

"But folks generally believe everyone is just like them until you do something that shakes that belief." Jimmy took another drink from his bottle of root beer. "I've had nearly twenty years to get used to the idea of supernaturals. Not everyone has had that grace."

"But the Rainier Outing was eleven years ago," Kaley protested. "It's not like the idea of the supernatural community is a new thing. Everyone had known unofficially Jo's a witch since she opened her café."

"But how often do we show off our abilities in public?" Kirsten said. Steam rose from the sink as she poured the fettucine into a strainer to drain the water. "Even Colin and Miz Anne were surprised to hear about Mom tossing a fireball in public."

"Fitz is already in town?" Jimmy said.

"Yeah, they got here a day early." Kirsten shook the strainer to get out the last drops of boiling water before she dumped the noodles back into the large saucepan. "We talked a bit after I drove Mary home."

"Which enforcer came with them?" Kaley asked.

"A new girl." Kirsten scooped the vegetables into the saucepan. "A Normal who's around our age named Ellie."

Jimmy's face turned white as the proverbial sheet. "Ellie Howell came with them?"

"No one gave me a last name when they made introductions at Joshua's farm." Kirsten poured the alfredo sauce over the vegetables and pasta. "Dinah called her Eleanor, but Colin and Miz Anne called her Ellie."

"Black hair, blue eyes, about yay-high." The sheriff held up his hand to indicate her height.

"Bit taller but that sounds like her. Kaley, would you grab the parmesan for me?" Kirsten picked up the wooden spoon Kaley had been using while sautéing the vegetables and mixed the ingredients in the sauce pan.

Kaley retrieved the canister from the fridge and handed it to Kirsten. "So, what's the issue with this Ellie?"

"She may be Normal, but she counts a god of war and a goddess of death as biological family," Jimmy said.

This Ellie sounded a little bit out there considering Kirsten's usual taste in friends. She generally avoided most other supernaturals. But this Normal who was a part of the vampire coven might be an interesting person to meet.

"She volunteered to help keep an eye on Jo's coffee shop," Kirsten said. She started dishing pasta into bowls.

"Who volunteered to watch Jo's shop?" Mom sauntered into the kitchen accompanied by the herbal scent of her homemade shampoo. She wore gray sweats and a white t-shirt with the slogan, "Editors do it 23.976/7".

Kaley grinned and ticked off their friends on her fingers. "So far we'll have three witches, one Amish, one fae, one werecoyote, the entire West Holmes girls' varsity basketball team, and now an enforcer from the St. James Vampire Coven when Jo opens in the morning."

Instead of looking pleased, Mom's expression became alarmed. "What's a St. James enforcer doing here?"

"Chill, honey." Dad reached for Mom, and she cuddled against his chest. It would be uncomfortably gross if it weren't for Kaley seeing how many of her friends' parents fought and split up. "Fitz and Anne are at Joshua Levy's place for Thanksgiving."

"And St. James isn't going to let Fitz see his family or Anne's without a guard," Jimmy added. "Especially not in Dare territory."

"I thought they weren't going to be here until tomorrow." Mom frowned, but she looked a little more relaxed from Dad's hug.

"The important thing is we've got people to keep the crazies at bay." Kaley distributed paper napkins and forks while her twin handed out the pasta primavera bowls. "It's not going to look good on the evening news in Cleveland or Columbus if those idiots throw rocks at a bunch of kids."

"The more important thing is I'll need a couple of extra deputies to watch the protestors." Jimmy shook his head at the situation as Kirsten set a bowl in front of him. He dug in with enthusiasm. After he chewed and swallowed, he added, "The commissioners aren't going to be happy if I go too far over budget this close to the end of the year."

"Do they really want these protestors destroying our town?" Mom snapped.

"No one wants that, but you and Jo threatening them with fireballs didn't help the situation." Jimmy glared right back at Mom.

"Those Humanity Now idiots would have hurt Kirsten if I hadn't done something!" Mom pulled free from Dad's hug. "And Pat Hall's people were nowhere in sight!"

"Mom!" Kaley and Kirsten said at the same time.

"Two policemen couldn't have taken on that mob by themselves," Kaley said.

"Not without someone getting hurt or killed," Kirsten added. "There's a zillion things that could've gone wrong, and Aunt Jo didn't help anything by charging out on the street and confronting Simon and his followers."

"From the mouths of babes," Dad murmured, but he was looking at Mom.

Her shoulders sagged, and she hugged herself. "You didn't see that crowd and the way they looked at our daughter, Ethan."

Dad stood. "You're right I didn't." He rested his hands on Mom's shoulders and looked her in the eye. "I probably would have done something worse. There's a reason I carry that cattle prod in my truck."

Mom snickered, and within a couple of seconds, they were all laughing at the ludicrous vision of Dad zapping the protestors.

But despite everyone's humor, Kaley had an uneasy feeling that something really bad was about to happen.

# Chapter 7

In the predawn dark the next morning, Kaley yawned in the passenger seat as Kirsten sped down the back roads to Joshua Levy's farm. Kaley leaned to the left to see the speedometer.

"Don't you think you should slow down a bit?"

"No," Kirsten snapped, but she eased up on the accelerator. "You know those jerks will be marching in front of the courthouse again."

"I know," Kaley said. "Why do you think I asked the guys to be there? Between coyote teeth and fae magick, we'll keep Jo inside the shop."

"What if they set the coffee shop on fire?" Kirsten murmured.

Her comment startled Kaley. While Kirsten was the more serious of the two of them, she was never that morbid. But then, Kaley had been uneasy herself since the text yesterday afternoon while she and River had been at the grocery store. The ominous sensation of impending doom settled over her again.

"What are you talking about?" Kaley said.

"I had nightmares last night," Kirsten murmured. "Different scenarios with Humanity Now. In one, they tossed Molotov cocktails through the windows and blocked the back door."

"Possible ways they're considering to kill us?" Kaley asked.

"Why does everyone expect me to be an oracle?"

"Because you're a water witch."

Kirsten groaned. "We're as bad at stereotyping ourselves as Normals doing it."

"Well, either you have a little precognitive talent or I do." Kaley stared at the dark fields they passed. "I've been on edge since yesterday."

"I like the idea of blaming you for my nightmares." Kirsten laughed.

"Bitch."

"It's better than being blond."

Kaley didn't respond to the old insult. Maybe it wasn't a psychic thing. Maybe Kirsten had seen something her subconscious recognized, but her conscious mind didn't. Or it could be as simple as her sister's primal fear when Simon knocked her to the pavement and the mob surged toward her.

Kirsten made the turn onto the Levys' drive. The Amish family's border collies charged off the back porch. The dogs were followed by two figures who approached the car. Something was off, but Kaley couldn't put her finger on it. Maybe it was leftover anxiety from yesterday's incident with Humanity Now.

She hoped.

Mary opened the rear door. Frigid air invaded the toasty warmth of the sedan. She slid into the back seat behind Kirsten. However, Kaley only got a glimpse of a dark leather jacket over a dark hoody before the other girl jumped into the back seat behind her. The slams of the two rear doors seemed terribly loud this early in the morning.

"You know I never realized how much goths and Amish had in common," she quipped.

"Ellie, the person making smartass comments too early in the morning is my sister, Kaley," Kirsten said. She shifted the gear into reverse and eased back down the driveway. The dogs pranced around like they were herding the sedan back to the paved road where it belonged.

So, this was the Normal enforcer accompanying Colin and Miz Anne.

"Hey," Ellie said, though the word sounded more like a groan. "Can I put in an order for three mochas with extra shots now?"

"A pleasure to meet you, Ms. Howell," Kaley said.

"Could you please not call me that?" Ellie growled. "It would be nice to be treated like a real Normal for once."

"You're an enforcer for a vampire covern," Kaley said. "That's not exactly normal Normal."

"You're both a talker and a morning person, aren't you?" Ellie said.

"Yep." The thing bothering Kaley at the farm clicked into place. "Mary, where's the family buggy?"

"Joshua said Father and Thomas needed help this morning," Mary said. "He didn't specify for what before he left."

Kaley's jaw dropped open as they drove down East Jackson Street. Streetlights showed every single parking spot was occupied by Amish buggies. Roughly, each third buggy held an Amish man bundled up against the morning's freezing temperatures. And each man held a cup with a familiar logo.

Two large sheets of plywood covered the huge broken window of Jo's coffee shop. However, the remaining window showed people inside. Lots of people, and not just their friends who volunteered to keep an eye on Jo's shop.

"She doesn't open until five," Kaley protested.

Kirsten turned into the parking lot behind the café. Only the space for the owner next to the dumpster was open.

"My aunt said the people here stick together against outsiders," Ellie said.

"Your aunt?" Kaley asked.

"Colin and Anne's youngest Sammi is named after her," Ellie added.

Kaley twisted to peer behind the seat. "And you can't say her name because . . ."

"You don't want the vampire's goddess of death to appear here," Mary said.

"C'mon, sis," Kirsten chided. "Uncle Jimmy pretty much said the same thing last night in our kitchen."

Kaley sighed as they all exited Mom's sedan. The other three were correct, and that only made her irritation worse. "My brain is still on Thanksgiving Break time."

Ellie laughed as they headed for the main doors of the café. "Don't feel bad. Mine is still on Thanksgiving Break Los Angeles Time."

Inside was controlled pandemonium. Hope Stillwell took orders and ran the register. Donny and Olivia Burke handled coffee and espresso while Jo made breakfast sandwiches and River bagged pastries.

The rest of the girls' varsity basketball team took up the two large tables by the unbroken window. A few of the Amish men sat along the smaller tables leading to the restrooms. The tables by the boarded-up window were occupied by English farmers and what Kaley referred to as the Old Fogies Club, a group of retired men who met here for breakfast every weekday that wasn't a holiday. That didn't count the dozen customer in line to give their breakfast orders.

"Aprons, ladies!" Jo yelled. "We need some help!"

Kaley followed Kirsten and Mary to the office. Ellie tagged along. They stowed coats and purses. Kirsten tossed an orange apron to Kaley. Mary was already putting on a black one.

"Got an extra apron?" Ellie asked. She had on a plain black t-shirt under the black hoodie and leather jacket she'd hung up on the coat pegs. It matched the black jeans and black boots she wore. Her equally dark hair was cropped at her chin, the kind of style that looked messy but cost beaucoup bucks at a high-end salon. Her hot pink nails had been professionally done as well. Black eyeliner and mascara framed her large blue eyes.

Kirsten nodded and handed over the one in her hand. She turned to grab another one from the clean pile on the shelf.

"You don't have to work here," Kaley said.

"It's better if I fit in with the rest of you," Ellie said. "If I look like another teen who works here, the Humanity Now assholes will underestimate me."

"You think they'd be dumb enough to try something else?" Kaley asked as they donned their aprons.

"Don't ever underestimate the meanness or stupidity of the average human being," Ellie answered.

The four of them trooped out of the office. Kaley replaced Hope at the register. The basketball team's center immediately went to the end of the order line. Olivia joined her a moment later as Kirsten started slinging coffee.

As Kaley suspected he would, Donny stayed at the the espresso station. Not when he had a chance to work next to his crush. She wasn't sure if Kirsten was that naïve or if she deliberately ignored the werecoyote's longing glances at her.

Without a word, Mary and Ellie split the dining area between them, collecting plates and cups from those who'd eaten in the café rather than getting breakfast to go and wiping down tables. For someone who probably never had to work a real job, much less waitress at a small-town coffee shop, Ellie Howell earned Kaley's respect.

River winked at her. She smiled back and logged into the system. As fast as Kaley took orders, the line never seemed to end.

"Good morning, Ms. Wilson." Police Chief Hall stood in front of her, wearing her uniform.

Kaley plastered on her customer service smile. "What can I get you, Chief?"

"A large non-fat mocha. No whip."

Kaley wrote the order on the paper cup and passed it to Donny. "Anything else?"

The chief lowered her voice. "Are you okay after what happened at the IGA yesterday?"

"How did you hear—"

"I got an earful from Shannon Murphy on the phone yesterday." Chief Hall's mouth tilted in a rueful smile.

Kaley groaned. "Not you, too. Uncle Jimmy stopped by our house after Shannon called him."

"He said there was someone else I needed to talk to here." The chief's attention flicked around the café.

"Take a wild guess." Kaley grinned.

Jo stepped closer. "Kaley, why don't you make introductions back in my office?"

With a start, Kaley looked out the remaining window. The sky was a soft blue, and sunlight bounced off the flagpole. "No problem."

She stepped away from the register. "Ellie?"

For all of her goth wear, the vampire coven enforcer had been friendly and charming to everyone at the café. It made Kaley wonder how much of Ellie's taste in clothing was her and how much was influenced by her employers.

Ellie's gaze flicked from Kaley to Chief Hall and back. Kaley inclined her head toward the back office. Ellie rolled her eyes. Was this why Mom and Dad got ticked off about that particular gesture?

Man, it *was* annoying.

Kaley marched back to Jo's office. A glance over her shoulder confirmed the chief and Ellie followed. Once they were inside with the door closed, Kaley made the introductions.

"I'm sorry, but why are you here, Ms. Howell?" Chief Hall cocked her head. "Jimmy told me we're in the middle of what the Dare Vampire Coven considers their territory."

"Because we have Family in Dare territory." Ellie crossed her arms. "It's a vampire thing. No one goes into another coven's territory without a guard."

"But a kid—" the chief started.

"I'm not a kid," Ellie bit out.

Chief Hall frowned. "How old are you?"

"I turned seventeen last month." Ellie yanked down the neck of the left side of her t-shirt. Ugly, jagged scars marred her pale skin at her shoulder. "I've been dealing with the things that go bump in the night before I was born." She released the black knit and shrugged her shirt back in place. "St. James Coven pays its debts. And we owe Josephine Bice and Rachel Wilson for their assistance in bringing the killer of one of our Family members to justice."

"The eye-for-eye thing doesn't fly in my town," Chief Hall stated.

Ellie held up her palms. "Nothing beyond a citizen's arrest. I promise." She smiled. "That doesn't mean I won't defend myself or my friends if someone swings first."

Chief Hall groaned. "I was hoping to get ahead of the supernatural problem."

Ellie laughed. "My mom says Murphy is the one true god."

Kaley stared at the enforcer. "Aren't you related to gods?"

"Don't remind me." Ellie waved at her t-shirt. "Where do you think my fashion taste comes from?"

Chief Hall chuckled. "Well, Matthew Yoder said pretty much the same thing about owing Jo and Rachel, but I generally don't have to worry about the Amish getting into a brawl."

"Jimmy said there would be some deputies assisting your officers today," Kaley said.

"Yes, there will be." Chief Hall frowned again. "I hope it's enough."

Kaley didn't want to say so, but part of her wondered if they had escalated the problem from the way her intuition itched.

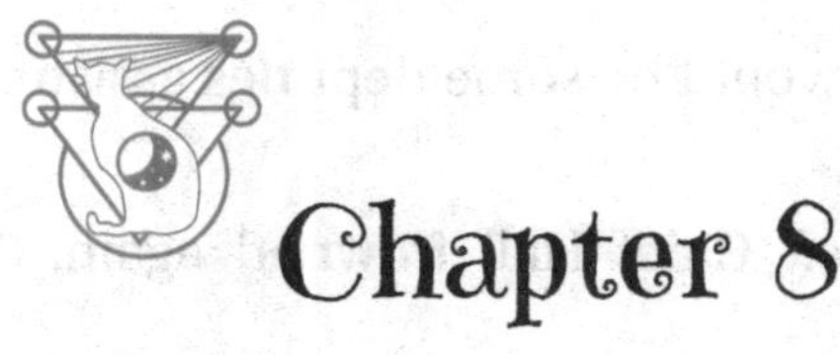

Chapter 8

Kirsten breathed a sigh of relief at five when she turned the sign indicating Jo's coffee shop was closed, and she locked the doors. Humanity Now had given up on their protest shortly after two. Their actions only showed their real reason to come to Millersburg was to harass Jo.

Some of the buggies left around three, but Mary's dad and brothers plus a handful of their friends remained. Kirsten didn't like the idea of the Amish staying in town so late. It would be full dark soon. However, Ellie called Anne at lunch. Apparently, Anne and Colin and their older children were helping with the farm chores of those who stayed in town.

The other thing bothering her was the reporter from Cleveland was back.

"Hope, did you get the name of the guy from *The Plain Dealer*?" Kirsten asked as they set the chairs upside down on the tables.

The tall blond appeared surprised. "You don't know Felix Finnegan? He's got a nationally syndicated column about the integration of supernaturals into American society."

"Did he say why he was here?"

Hope made a disgusted expression. "Just that he was doing a series about Humanity Now. I told him maybe he needed to take a real look at the people being harassed, instead of the idiots my mother has been hanging out with." She paused and looked at Kirsten. "I hope you don't think I agree with Mom's crap."

"You wouldn't be here if you did." Kirsten smiled.

"I was so frickin' mad when she came home, claiming your mom tried to set people on fire." Hope shook her head as she flipped another chair onto the table she worked on. "David lit into her about the sacrifices he, our brothers, and his friends made overseas so everyone could live in peace here. He was about ready to go back to his base instead of spending the rest of his leave at home. By the way, if he and Dad get the grain elevator running by tonight, David's coming with me here to the café tomorrow."

"That would be awesome." Kirsten grinned. If a decorated marine couldn't convince the protesters they were acting foolishly, nothing could.

Mary and Ellie mopped the dining area while Hope and Kirsten helped Jo and the other four kids finish cleaning the kitchen. Everything was done in record time with the extra help. Jo paid Donny, River, Hope, and Olivia for their temporary help today, but when it came to Ellie, the girl refused the cash.

"But you spent the entire day here," Jo said. "You worked your ass off."

"And you gave me multiple mochas, not to mention lunch." Ellie waved her hand. "I count us even."

Her attitude didn't surprise Kirsten. Despite her casual appearance, her clothes were tailored, and her leather coat and boots probably cost more than Dad paid for the '67 Electra Kirsten and her sister were helping him restore. Ellie was probably a trust fund baby, but she already said she liked being here because no one knew who she was.

Or how much money her family had.

"You want a ride back to the farm?" Kaley asked.

Ellie shook her head. "Mary and I will catch a lift with Joshua. Though we wouldn't mind if you pick us up in the morning."

Mary glared at the enforcer. "You shouldn't take advantage of their kindness to us."

"It's too cold at four-thirty in the morning for a buggy ride," Ellie shot back. "And frankly, us California girls are not used to this weather."

"No worries, guys." Kaley gestured at the surrounding area. "We can pick you up."

"What she means is I'll pick you up while she sleeps on the way to Joshua's farm." Kirsten handed Kaley her varsity jacket.

Kaley stuck her tongue out at Kirsten.

Ellie grabbed Kaley's sleeve. "What the hell sliced up your coat?"

Kaley sighed and examined the tears on the leather. "One of the kids in town is a dreamwalker. He has a little trouble controlling his powers."

One of Ellie's dark eyebrows rose. "And he went all movie slasher on the pretty blond cheerleader in his nightmares?"

"No, he thought werecoyotes are awesome." Donny grinned. "Which we are."

"It was an accident," Kaley said. "I haven't had time to patch my jacket."

Kirsten nibbled on her lower lip. Maybe this was why both she and her sister had the heebie-jeebies the last few days. Noah Eisler was a kid who didn't understand what he was doing or what was happening when he slept. River's mom was mentally ill and hoped to turn the citizens of Millersburg against the fae after his dad seduced then abandoned her to raise River alone.

But the incident yesterday with Humanity Now?

That wasn't about someone in trouble. It was people causing trouble out of hate.

And that wasn't a problem solved by a spell.

Heavy clouds darkened the sky much earlier than sunset. As they walked out to their cars. Kaley tugged Kirsten's jacket sleeve.

Don't make it obvious, but behind us. Across the street by the corner of the courthouse.

Luckily, Aunt Jo walked behind them.

Kirsten looked over her shoulder. "What time are we closing tomorrow, Jo? We need to get our holiday tree." She focused and really Looked at the man Kaley had spotted. He was a Normal, but his aura had a dark red hue. It didn't appear like the brick red outline of a vampire though.

"One p.m.," Jo said. "I've got some baking of my own to do before Thursday."

"See you in the morning then!" Kirsten waved before they rounded the corner of the building. She hit the button on the fob to unlock the doors.

Once she and Kaley were inside Mom's sedan, Kirsten silently said, *What about him besides the stain on his aura?*

He's the guy who was talking to Mrs. Ryder in the IGA parking lot yesterday.

Kirsten buckled up and hit the ignition button. She backed out of the parking spot and drove toward the exit into the alley that ran behind the coffee shop. After a left turn to reach the cross street, she turned right as the first drops of rain hit their windshield.

"Going a little out of our way, aren't we?" Kaley said.

"Call me paranoid." Kirsten checked all the mirrors. There was no one behind them. "You think he's with Humanity Now?"

"A distinct possibility." Kaley clicked her tongue against her teeth. "He didn't look happy when River and I drove past him. Mrs. Ryder had to find out about the confrontation between Mom and the protesters from someone who was there. She got in my face about five minutes after your text."

"You know that weird feeling we've both been having?"

"Yeah." Kaley drawled.

"I don't think its straight precognition. I think something has already been set in motion, and Humanity Now is involved."

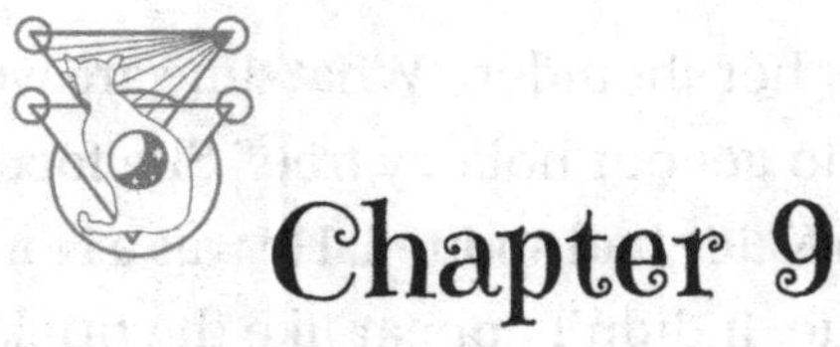

Chapter 9

While they were preparing dinner, Kaley asked Mom if air witches were ever precognitive.

Mom shook her head. "Not that I've ever heard of. Why?"

"I've been having a weird feeling since Monday. I wasn't sure if it was me or if I was picking up something from Kirsten." Kaley popped a chunk of the carrot she was slicing into her mouth.

"Kirsten's having premonitions?" Mom set the pan filled with the garlic and potatoes in water on the front left stove burner and flipped on the gas. After two clicks, blue flames hugged the base of the pan. Mom turned down the heat.

"No," Kaley said as she set aside the paring knife. "I asked her. She said she's just worried about Humanity Now after what happened yesterday. But maybe you should close the *Monitor*'s office tomorrow to play it safe."

Mom chuckled before she crossed the kitchen and hugged Kaley. "You're as bad as your father. But to reassure you girls, I'm planning to work from home tomorrow, and I told the rest of my staff to do the same. Does that make you feel better?"

"Loads." Kaley grinned.

The next morning, Dad insisted Kaley and her sister take his pickup if they were going to get a holiday tree after work, and he'd take Mom's sedan to the clinic. After the twins picked up Mary and Ellie and returned to town, they all looked at each other in surprise. Local English farmers and their pickups lined Jackson Street for three blocks in every direction from the courthouse corner. Hope Stillwell and her brother David rushed around inside the café with Jo, prepping for the customers waiting patiently outside in the cold and windy weather.

Kaley prayed things would be as quiet downtown as they had been yesterday. While the others donned their aprons, Jo let in the customers on the sidewalk. She handed a pad and pen to Kaley.

"Take orders from everyone in the pickups. Their drinks are on the house." Jo frowned. "But if you see even one Humanity Now idiot, get your butt back in here, and let Pat's people deal with it."

Kaley glanced across the street. Sure enough, a team consisting of a police officer, a sheriff's deputy, and a Brown Dog enforcer patrolled around the courthouse and the historic jail. Two other teams strode up and down Jackson, their attention hooked on every vehicle and pedestrian that rolled or walked by them. Chief Enforcer Lambert obviously called in reinforcements. Had the Dare Coven's chief enforcer John Robbins called in more of his people, too?

Most of the varsity girls' basketball team showed up while Kaley took orders. Every one of the farmers ordered food when she informed them their coffees, teas, and hot chocolates were free. All of them tipped way more than the standard gratuity.

David assisted Kaley in taking breakfasts out to the folks standing guard, much to River's dismay. It wasn't like David flirted with her or anything. He treated Kaley just like he did his baby sister.

Kaley couldn't deny David was attractive with his height, muscles, and sun-bleached locks. But he was also ten years older than her and currently married to the Marine Corps, though Hope hinted he'd been dating a nurse during his last deployment overseas.

Olivia Burke and Angie Matlow rushed into the café a little after six.

"Sorry, we're late," Angie said. Olivia stormed back to the office, which was totally unlike her.

"What's going on?" Kaley murmured. She could feel Kirsten, River, and Donny listening to the conversation through her.

"Olivia's dad didn't want her coming here after he heard about the confrontation between Humanity Now and your family." Angie shrugged. "He threatened to ground her. Then her mom jumped in and started yelling at him about how his grandmother was an activist for Black rights back in the day. They weren't paying any attention to us, so we slipped out of the house."

"Goddess help us," Kaley whispered. "I hope Olivia knows what she's doing."

"So do I." Angie grinned. "That's one thing I like about my parents getting divorced. They're too busy fighting with each other to pay any attention to me."

Thankfully, Olivia's issues with her parents were the only excitement. None of the Humanity Now protesters showed up. Not with all the farmers' hunting rifles on display in their pickups' gun racks.

Jo closed the coffee shop at one p.m. sharp as she promised. Donny rode with the twins while they dropped off Mary and Ellie at the Levy homestead. The trio then headed for the Slaughter's Christmas tree farm to get trees for both of their households.

Kaley trudged after Kirsten and Donny through the rows of white pines. Thank Goddess, she'd brought her rubber boots. Despite her wishful thinking, last night's rain did not turn to snow. Instead, it created aisles of mud between the trees. River refused to come with them. Something about he couldn't stand to hear the trees scream when they were cut down.

Mom, Dad, and Donny's mother deemed the outing safe. The

Humanity Now people didn't show up at all in front of the court-house this morning. It didn't make sense why they bothered to march at all during the week of Thanksgiving.

Well, other than to bring down everyone else's holiday.

"Do you guys smell something funky?" Donny said.

Kaley sniffed the air. "All I smell is pine."

"Me, too," Kirsten added. "You sure it's not cow patties from the pasture next door."

"No." Donny inhaled deeply. "It's meat rotting."

"We don't have your werecoyote senses," Kirsten said. "It could be a dead bird under one of the trees. Or a dead squirrel."

"Why do you automatically go to the gross stuff?" Kaley snapped.

"I'm not the one who detected a dead critter." Kirsten pointed over to the next row with her gloved hand holding their saw. "Let's check that row."

Kaley slid around on the path as she followed the other two. The ground was more slippery in her boots than Matt Jessup's frozen pond in ice skates.

"The smell's stronger over here," Donny complained.

"Then let's pick a tree and get out of here," Kirsten said.

"What about this one?" Donny stood next to a tree that was a foot taller than him. The bottom of the pine was so wide its lowest branches interlocked with its neighbors.

"Looks good to me." Kirsten brandished their saw. "Whatcha think, K?"

"Let me check the other side," Kaley said.

"Why do you get so picky?" Donny complained.

"Because Mom and Dad like to do the Victorian thing in our semi-Victorian house," Kaley shot back. "Which means the dang tree has to look good from both inside the house and from the side-walk outside."

She pushed past the left branches. Her right foot caught on

something in the mulch, and she pitched forward. Cold and wet soaked through the knees of her jeans and her mittens upon her landing.

"Gross!"

"You okay?" Kirsten yelled.

"I tripped over a damn root." Kaley kicked in an attempt to free her foot only to lose her dang boot. She cursed under her breath. Now, mud soaked into her sock as well as her jeans. The walk back to the pickup and the ride home were going to be uncomfortable, cold, and messy.

She reached for the root trapping the toe of her boot, but it wasn't rough bark that met her hand. It felt more like heavy duck cloth. She sat up in the mud. Did someone lose a jacket out here?

Another yank freed her boot, but along with the jacket sleeve, a hand popped out of the mix of mulch, mud, and needles.

"K-kirsten!" Kaley swallowed hard.

Kirsten pushed her way past the branches on the other side of the tree Donny had picked out. "What's wrong?"

Kaley could only point. Death wasn't something she shirked from. She had helped Dad at the clinic when he had to put down other families' pets. But this was a human being.

Donny stepped toward her and held up the lowest branches for a better look. Kirsten scraped away the mud and mulch with the edge of the saw from the blueish hand and brown material until she found a face. The hand and duck cloth sleeve were connected to a man. A dead man.

Warren Simon.

"Told you guys I smelled something rotten," Donny grumbled.

Chapter 10 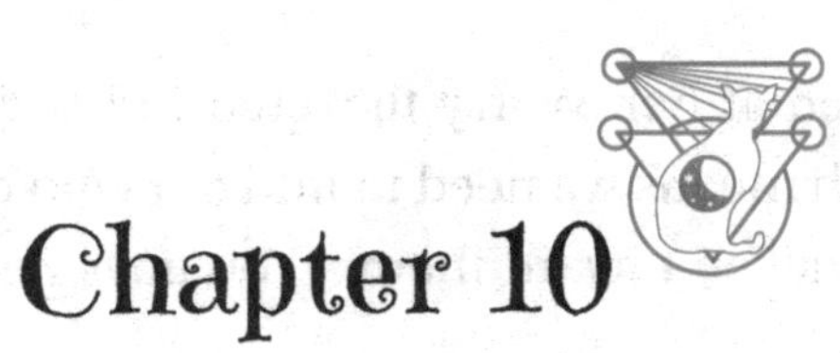

Clouds darkened the sky, blocking any hint of sunshine and threatening more rain. Kirsten hugged herself and watched while the sheriff and deputies took pictures of the dead man. Kaley sat inside Dad's pickup, wrapped in a blanket, and perched on a trash bag to keep from smearing mud all over the upholstery.

"Maybe you should get inside the truck and warm up," Donny said softly. He stood next to her watching the activity. The deputies had originally separated the three of them for questioning, but with last night's rain, it was obvious the body had been under the tree for a while.

"I need to get used to this," Kirsten muttered. "Especially if I'm going to start interning with law enforcement next year."

"You have to get used to freezing?" He looked at her as if she were insane.

Maybe she was.

"No." She shook her head. "Seeing a dead body."

"Like Millersburg has that many suspicious deaths." He lowered his voice. "We may have a different problem."

"What?"

"There was a hell of a lot of ozone around the body."

A shiver ran up her spine that had nothing to do with the current weather. "Honey or ginger?"

"Couldn't pick up anything with the rotten meat smell mixed with pine, rain, and mud." He snorted. "Especially not with Kaley tripping over the body."

Kirsten swore under her breath. "You realize my family is going to be the prime suspects?"

He looked at her. Worry flickered in his golden eyes. "Yeah, I know. Which means we need to find out who did this. And fast."

Jimmy stalked toward them. "You guys need to come down to headquarters."

"Can we call our parents?" Donny asked. "Let them know where we are?"

"I already had Joy call them," Jimmy said. Joy Bridges was the head dispatcher for the sheriff's department. Kirsten tried not to react. Mom would beat them to the brick building the Holmes County Sheriff's Department called home.

And she'd be raising one hell of a ruckus.

"Do we need to ride with the deputies?" Kirsten waved in the direction of Dad's pickup. "Kaley's covered in mud."

"Actually, I want you to ride with me." He gestured at Donny. "Give Fryer your keys."

Oh, crap on a cracker. Of course, Jimmy wanted to speak with her first. She'd been the one Simon knocked to the pavement during Monday afternoon's confrontation.

Kirsten reached into her front jeans pocket and pulled out the key ring for the truck. She dropped the keys into Donny's palm. "Not a scratch on it, or I will curse you with the worst case of fleas you've ever experienced."

He grinned. "What do I get for safely delivering both the truck and your sister to the sheriff?"

She shook her head at his teasing. "First, tell Sheriff Birkheimer exactly what you just told me." This was an official investigation. It would be best if she addressed her godfather by his title.

Jimmy's expression turned puzzled. "What did you pick up?"

Donny sobered fast. "Ozone. A lot of it. A major spell had to be cast on Simon for it to still be there after last night's storm."

"Witch or fae?" the sheriff asked.

"Can't tell over dead Normal." Donny shrugged.

Suspicion flashed in Jimmy's dark eyes.

Donny spread his hands wide. "Hey, if I knew, I'd tell you and Kirsten. The last thing we need is someone retaliating on that jerk. Even I get how bad that looks."

Jimmy continued to glare at Donny. "All right, but we need to have a little talk about you withholding information, Mr. Fryer."

"Yes, sir." At least, it sounded like a respectful acknowledgement, not Donny's usual sarcastic crap.

Kirsten followed Jimmy to his official SUV. When she paused by the door to the back seat, he shook his head.

"You're not under arrest. Not yet, anyway."

She swallowed hard and moved to the front passenger seat. Once she settled in the vehicle and buckled her seatbelt, he threw the SUV into gear and performed a J-turn.

"Thanks for getting Donny to cough up the info," he murmured when he pulled onto the pavement of the township road.

"In all honesty, he didn't mention the ozone scent to me until right before you approached us," she said.

"I kinda figured from the sour look on your face." A small smile graced his features.

"Do you really think I killed Simon, or are you covering your bases?"

Jimmy chuckled. "You sound more like your mother every day."

"Oka-a-ay." Kirsten wasn't sure where he was going with this. But then, it wasn't like her mother to do a public magick display either. Everything in her life had turned topsy-turvy lately.

"It wasn't an insult, Kirsten." He glanced at her before returning his attention to the road. "If Jo or your mother had committed the murder, they know how to hide the body. Or they would've called someone from Brown Dog to help them dispose of it."

Kirsten stared at her godfather. His statement wasn't mean. More . . . matter-of-fact. Like Mom and Jo and he had been in such a position before this. She never considered her family or Jimmy Birkheimer as people who thought themselves above the law.

"Is that what you guys had to do with someone?" she asked tentatively.

He glanced at her again. "If Thad Wolford hadn't followed Miz Anne's supernatural enforcer protocols, Fitz would be sitting in the Marion Correctional Facility for whacking off a guy's head. Do you think Fitz shouldn't have defended himself? Do you think Jo shouldn't have helped capture the other fae? Do you think Leslie Warner should be behind bars for killing Donny's dad?"

Those were the same questions Kaley had asked Kirsten years ago. Kaley's rhetorical queries had followed after Kirsten questioned Donny's chip on his shoulder after a run-in with a couple of members of the Killbuck Pack at Dairy Queen. Kaley continued by asking Kirsten whether Donny should be punished for what his dad had done. Chad Fryer had sided with the Winter Queen's assassin. According to Mom and Jo, he'd kidnapped two of Leslie's children and threatened to kill them.

"It sounds like you don't think much of the old supernatural legal system," Kirsten commented.

"In some ways, it's probably more just than the Normal system," Jimmy said. "In other ways, it's scary as all get out."

"So, why am I riding with you?"

"How do I know if a spell killed Warren Simon?"

She stared out the windshield. The clouds had broken to the west. Venus showed above the glow along the horizon. "You're going to need to get a witch enforcer here."

"Why can't you tell me?"

"Because one, I'm not that far in my studies yet, and two, do you really think the prosecutor isn't going to rip my testimony apart?" she snapped. "Warren Simon assaulted me two days ago, and now my twin sister just so happens to trip over his body while we're picking out holiday trees?"

"I'm not the enemy here, kiddo," he murmured.

"I'm sorry if that came out wrong, but I understand you have to do your job."

"It's good to know you're thinking logically about this," he added.

"Why?"

"Because I've already made some calls. A couple more coven enforcers are on their way here."

Chapter 11

Kaley wiggled in an attempt to find a spot on her rear that didn't ache. Her chair in the sheriff's interrogation room was beginning to feel more like rock than plastic. It didn't help that the mud caked on her jeans was drying and left chunks of dirt all around her chair.

She obeyed Mom's silent command not to say anything until she and Dad got to the sheriff's office. It didn't stop Detective Lyle Mercer from staring daggers at her.

The door swung open, but the man with Mom wasn't Dad.

Colin Fitzgerald smiled at the detective. "Hey, Lyle. I'd like to speak with my client privately."

"Have you really kept your Ohio license, Fitz?" Detective Mercer pushed back from the table and stood. The two men shook hands.

"It was a lot easier to do when I didn't need much sleep, but yes, I have." They released each other, and they both turned and looked at Kaley.

Mom rushed over and hugged her tight. "Are you all right, sweetie?"

"Other than sitting in mud-soaked jeans after tripping over a dead man, I'm just peachy." She glared at the detective.

"Your dad is in the waiting area with some clean clothes." Mom glared at Detective Mercer, too. "I believe our lawyer asked you to leave, Lyle."

"You don't have to be a bitch about things, Rachel." But the detective reached for the door handle. "But it's in your kids' best interest to cooperate."

"I'm representing Donny Fryer as well as the Wilson girls." Colin grinned at the detective. "So don't try an end run around with the other two kids."

Detective Mercer grunted and left the room.

Tears stung Kaley's eyes when Mom sat next to her and asked again, "Are you okay?"

"Other than cold, damp, muddy jeans and throwing up after I realized it wasn't a root or a branch my boot was caught on, I'm fine." Kaley looked at Colin. "They can't really believe we killed Warren Simon."

"According to both Kirsten and Mary, there was a confrontation between your family and Simon on Monday." Colin sat down on the chair Detective Mercer had vacated.

"Which was instigated by Simon!" Mom waved her hands in the air.

Colin grimaced. "The sheriff's department and the county prosecutor will have to hang Kirsten out to dry if anyone else in the family is found to have been involved."

Mom's shoulders sagged.

Kaley looked at her and back at Colin. "They can't do that! She tried to stop the screaming match between Jo and Simon!"

"They can, and they will if they have to." Colin blew out a deep breath. "Where were you between eleven last night and when you tripped over Simon's body?"

This was ridiculous, but Kaley answered the lawyer. "I was in bed by nine. Asleep until my alarm went off at four. Got dressed. Kirsten and I picked up Mary and Ellie at Joshua's farm around four-thirty and got to Jo's coffee shop by ten to five. We all worked until Jo closed at one. Donny came with us to drop off Mary and Ellie at the farm, and me, Kirsten and Donny went straight to the Slaughter's tree farm."

Colin looked up at Mom. "And where were you during those same hours, Mrs. Wilson?"

"What's that supposed to mean?" Mom crossed her arms and scowled at the lawyer.

"It means we need an alibi for every single member of your family, Rachel." He jabbed his index finger in the general direction of the coffee shop. "You were the ones last seen having a public beef with the dead guy."

Mom opened her mouth when Detective Mercer and another deputy charged into the room. "Rachel Wilson, you are under arrest."

Chapter 12

Kaley jumped to her feet. "What are you talking about?"

"Hands behind your back." Detective Mercer had a set of hand-cuffs in his grip.

"Wait a minute here, Lyle." Colin rose to his full height, probably because he was a couple of inches taller than the detective. "What's the charge?"

"Murder," Detective Mercer said grimly. "Kaley, it's best if you leave. Your dad is waiting for you out in reception."

Kaley swallowed hard. "That's impossible." She turned to Colin. "Tell him Mom couldn't have done it. She wouldn't hurt anybody."

Colin circled the table and clasped her shoulder. "Do as Detective Mercer asks, Kaley. I'll stay here with your mother." He glared at the detective. "I'll get this straightened out as soon as I can."

Kaley walked out of the interrogation room, her chest aching. Three days ago, she would have bet her life Mom would never use her powers in public, much less harm someone.

And now?

The video being spread across the county made her question everything Mom had taught her.

Kirsten leaned against the slightly sticky wall. She tried not to think about what made it sticky. The ache in her butt helped distract her. The hardwood bench wasn't meant to be napped on, much less perched on for a couple of hours.

Part of her wanted to cry with relief when Mom and Dad arrived with Colin. For all of her desire to leave small town life, the responsibilities of adulthood were too damn heavy at the moment. She'd dealt with dead animals before at Dad's clinic and when she accompanied him on farm calls, but this was so very different. However, an average witch's lifespan was roughly fifty years longer than a Normal's. Grandma and Grandpa Wilson were in pretty good health for being Normal. It wasn't like any of the immediate family had been to a funeral since she and her sister were babies.

But Kirsten couldn't stop her mind from replaying the scene at the pine tree farm—Kaley sprawled in the mud and the blueish hue of Warren Simon's hand clutching the toe of her sister's boot. Or rather the corpse's hand.

Dad sat next to her on the bench. He propped Kaley's overnight bag next to him and wrapped his arm around Kirsten's shoulders. Colin and Mom had a few loud words with the desk sergeant before he buzzed them through and they charged down the hallway. A few minutes later, Detective Mercer stormed out of the same hallway and used his key card to enter the office section.

Thankfully, Dad didn't say a word. Kirsten leaned against his chest, and they sat quietly on the stupid bench until his phone beeped. He pulled it out of his pocket and checked the message.

"I'm sorry, sweetheart," he murmured. "I have to take this."

She nodded mutely. He stood, kissed her on the forehead before he strode out one of the main doors. Damn, she missed the comfort he gave her.

Donny came out of his interrogation a few minutes later. He stalked toward her bench and flopped next to her.

"Aren't your parents here?" he asked.

"Mom and Colin Fitzgerald are with Kaley," she said. "Dad got a message and stepped out to return the call."

"At least you've got someone who came," he muttered.

"Did you call your mom?"

"Yeah." He blew out a harsh breath. "She couldn't leave work."

"I'm sorry." And she was. It wasn't fair she had two parents with careers. It wasn't fair Donny's dad acted stupid and got himself killed by another werecoyote. It wasn't fair Donny's mom worked two jobs to raise him. He looked so damn dejected sitting beside her.

No, none of this was fair.

"I hope this doesn't screw up your scholarship." She wrapped her hand around his. Donny froze for an instant, but he slowly curled his fingers around hers.

"That's assuming I get to keep it," he murmured.

"What?"

He leaned against the sticky wall, too. "You know the lawsuit over the NCAA allowing supernaturals on teams?"

"Yeah?" she said cautiously.

"I got a letter from the university yesterday. My scholarship has been put on hold, pending a review by the legal department."

"Oh, Goddess," she breathed. This was worse than she thought.

"Yeah, even after working my ass off over the last five summers, there's no way I can pay for my first year of college, much less all four."

Kirsten's eyes stung. She squeezed his hand. Donny squeezed back before he chuckled.

"Funny thing is now football season's done, I had an alibi for last night."

She turned her head to look at him. "But you only worked at Jo's until five yesterday."

"I was at the Dyrty Byrd at seven to grab something to eat before my shift started at eight," he said. "Hank, Mom, and I were the last out of the bar at three this morning, and Hank talked to Deputy Collins when I called Mom. He told the deputy he's got the security video from last night to show I was there." He frowned and lowered his voice. "Since the rain started about five p.m., the sheriff's people seem pretty sure Simon was murdered and dumped at the Slaughters' place before then."

"I honestly don't know how you keep up with everything on your plate." Kirsten shook her head. "Did you even sleep?"

"Just a catnap after I took a shower." Donny grinned at his bad joke.

She sighed. "I was dead to the world by nine last night. Unfortunately, that only leaves my family as my alibi."

Detective Mercer charged out of the administrative hallway he'd disappeared down a few minutes ago. He muttered something to the desk sergeant before he continued back toward the interrogation room. The one where Kaley was with Mom and Colin. The detective appeared even more unhappy than when Colin kicked him out a little bit ago.

A couple of minutes later, Kaley stumbled out into the reception area.

Kirsten and Donny released each other's hands and stood.

Dad strode back into the building. "Kaley?"

She burst into tears and ran into Dad's arms. "Mom's been arrested!"

Kirsten felt as if someone had punched her in the gut. Donny wrapped his arm around her waist and held her up when her knees buckled. His action reminded her just how strong he was.

"Where's Fitz?" Dad growled.

"He-he's still in the interrogation room with Mom and the detective," Kaley said between sobs.

Dad stalked toward the door to the interrogation rooms.

Kaley's fear intensified as she picked up the raw power that slammed into hers and Kirsten's mental shields. There was a vampire right outside of the building that housed the sheriff's department and the county jail.

The desk sergeant jumped up and held out a hand. "You can't go back there, Doc."

"I want to see my wife," Dad snapped. He looked like he was about to push the sergeant aside.

Kirsten raced over and inserted herself between the men. "Stop it, Dad. Don't make Kaley and me bail both our parents out of jail," she said both out loud and silently.

He jumped and glared at her.

She hadn't used her telepathy on Dad since she was a toddler, and back then, her voice in his mind scared the crap out of him. It was the only time he'd been truly uncomfortable when it came to hers and Kaley's witch powers. But in his rage right now, she could Hear he was about to do something very, very stupid.

Dad, for the love of the Goddess, listen to me this once. Let Colin do his job. If we do this the wrong way, it'll make things a lot worse for Mom.

He took a step back from her, like she knew he would do, and stared at her. "Don't ever do that again, young lady."

"Then don't pick a fight with a law officer," she said as calmly as she could.

"You should listen to your daughter, Doctor Wilson," said a female voice.

This time, Kirsten was the one to nearly jump out of her skin. She hadn't Heard the two new people enter through the main entrance. Brown Dog's chief enforcer Jill Lambert swept toward them.

Chief Enforcer Lambert was a tall woman, easily matching Hope's six-feet without the two-inch heels on her boots. She wore a black wool pantsuit underneath her tan trench coat. A mulberry scarf that matched the shade of her hair was wrapped around her neck. Kirsten had seen the man accompanying the chief enforcer when she and Kaley had been formally inducted into the coven, but she didn't remember being introduced to him.

"I'm Jill Lambert," the chief enforcer said to the desk sergeant. "Sheriff Birkheimer called me in for a case consultation."

The desk sergeant nodded. "One moment, Chief Enforcer." He turned back to Dad. "You gonna behave yourself, Doc?"

Kirsten crossed her fingers nothing else would go wrong. Dad nodded stiffly, and the sergeant relaxed. While he called back to the sheriff's office within the building, the chief enforcer stepped closer to Dad.

"Go home, Doctor Wilson." She shot a sympathetic look toward Kaley who still had tears streaming down her cheeks before she looked at Dad again. "Take your daughters home and feed them. Enforcer Tyler and I will stay here. Chief Enforcer Robbins is on his way."

Dad went rigid again. "Why him?"

"Because Jimmy Birkheimer trusts him." Chief Enforcer Lambert tilted her head as she regarded Dad. "Is your reluctance about Robbins's disease?"

"No," Dad spat. "I have issues because my family assisted a St. James enforcer nearly twenty years ago, and I know there's no love lost between them and Dare Coven."

Lambert raised one mulberry eyebrow. "Don't you have a St. James attorney in with your wife right now?"

"That's part of my concern," Dad stated. "Besides, he's Normal."

"Now, he's Normal, you mean," she pointed out.

Dad spluttered a bit, but Kirsten put her hands on his chest. "Please, Dad. Let's go home. If not for Mom's sake, then for Kaley's. She's had a rough day."

"You should go home, too. Kirsten, right?" Lambert said.

Kirsten knew why the chief enforcer made that suggestion. Every witch in the building could feel the raw power of Chief Enforcer Robbins outside in the parking lot. He was deliberately announcing his presence. And it explained why Chief Enforcer Lambert was trying to get Dad to go home. She didn't need more problems on top of a member of Brown Dog being arrested for the murder of a Normal.

"No, Kirsten and Donny are staying here for just a little bit longer." Uncle Jimmy addressed Lambert as he strode out of the hallway leading to the offices. "They have some information you and the other enforcers need to hear. Do you two have a ride home when we're done?"

"Yes, sir." Kirsten fished the truck keys from her pocket and held them out to Dad. "Mom's not going to want dried mud all over the interior of her car."

"And I do?" Dad gave her an odd look, but he exchanged the sedan fob for his truck keyring.

"There's already mud in the truck." Kirsten shrugged. "We did our best with the garbage bags. I promise I'll clean out your truck this weekend."

He didn't argue further. "Don't keep the kids too late, Jimmy. They've been working all day, every day, at Jo's this week."

"I know," the sheriff said. "And I won't."

Dad wrapped his arm around Kaley, and they left.

"What's going on?" Kirsten asked.

"Chief Enforcer Robbins is waiting for your dad to pull out of the parking lot," Jimmy replied. Of course, the vampire was. It got dark pretty early this time of year.

"Ah, crap," Kirsten muttered. "Did he hear what Dad said?"

"Yes," Lambert said. "He was talking to me when your father was speaking." She smiled at Kirsten. "Don't worry. John isn't taking it personally. That's part of the reason he's here instead of another Dare enforcer."

"Don't worry, Kirsten." Jimmy smiled. "John's the last person to dredge up old grudges. Also, I asked him to pick up Anne on the way over here."

Kirsten tensed, and Lambert frowned.

"Are you insane? Are you trying to start a war?" Enforcer Tyler stared at Jimmy.

"What happened to my request for cooperation?" he shot back. "Besides, this isn't the first time, Anne and John have worked together."

"C'mon, Sheriff!" Donny laughed. "You know the other supers don't behave themselves unless a certain goddess makes them."

"Donny, are you crazy?" Kirsten stared at him. She knew he could do some stupid stuff to prove himself, but he wouldn't actually summon *her* here, would he?

"Mr. Fryer has a point." Jimmy folded his arms over his chest. "And I'm not above calling out the big guns if you folks are going to get into a pissing contest over jurisdiction. I politely asked for your assistance. If you can't do that, then every enforcer needs to leave."

"Relax, Jimmy," a smooth male voice came from the doorway. "You don't need a cannon to kill an ant."

Kirsten turned toward the main doors into headquarters. The tall man with Anne Levy-Fitzgerald and Ellie Howell had to be the vampire she sensed outside the building from the brick red outline to his aura. His sharp nose and high cheekbones indicated Native American, which was why his skin didn't have the awful paleness of Caucasians with the V-virus. He wore jeans and a hunting jacket with sturdy boots that had seen some use.

"Can we get started?" Chief Enforcer Robbins said. "I don't want to be here longer than necessary because I know what happens to my people after a white folks Thanksgiving."

Chapter 13

Kaley leaned against the pickup door, the glass of the passenger window cooling her hot face. Headlights from oncoming vehicles whooshed by, but she wasn't sure if they were speeding or if Dad was. She didn't have the energy to lift her head and check the speedometer.

"I'm sorry, sweetheart," Dad murmured. "Finding that guy had to have scared the hell out of you."

"The real problem was having to pee, and the deputies not letting me go to the bathroom after all the coffee I drank this morning," she muttered.

"What?" Dad's outrage was back.

"Don't sweat it, Dad." She sighed. "Jimmy made them let me go to the ladies room. I just wish we'd gotten our holiday trees before we found the body."

"Next week, we'll go somewhere else to pick out trees for us and the Fryers," Dad assured her. "Once we get things with your mom squared away. Right now, let's get you home and fed."

Kaley laughed though it sounded weak to her own ears. "The only thing you can make without burning it is scrambled eggs and bacon."

"We can stop anywhere you like, sweetheart."

"Actually, eggs and bacon with some toast sounds pretty good." She sighed again. "All I ask is I get a shower first. I swear I have mud in every crevice."

"No problem, sweetheart." Dad reached over and patted her one knee that wasn't caked with drying mud. "No problem at all."

Kaley toweled her hair dry as she shuffled to her bedroom. Penn and Teller were still curled around each other on her pale pink comforter like a muted yin-yang symbol. She checked her phone. A few texts from other high school friends, but not one damn text or call from River.

Maybe he was doing some chores for his grandmother. Maybe he had fallen asleep after getting up well before dawn to help at Jo's coffee shop. Maybe she'd totally misread his signals.

No, he assured her that he and his grandmother were coming over for dinner—

Goddess! Tomorrow was Thanksgiving.

Despite the weariness attempting to drag her into bed with the cats, she pulled on clean jeans and a sweatshirt, twisted her damp hair into a messy knot, and clipped it in place before she headed downstairs. The savory scent of bacon greeted her long before she stepped foot into the kitchen.

Dad looked up from the stove. "Jo called while you were in the shower. She asked if you would give her a call back tonight."

"Did you tell her about the dead guy and Mom?"

"Yes. She promised not to do anything stupid." Dad grimaced as he filled their plates with scrambled eggs. "Though I think it's more because Fitz is representing her than anything I said. Thank goodness he kept his Ohio law license active after he moved to Los Angeles."

The toaster popped with four slices. At the scent, Kaley's stomach rumbled in a way that if River were here, she would be turning bright red.

She crossed to the refrigerator, opened its door, and retrieved the butter and blueberry jam. While she pulled out the toast, Dad added bacon to their plates and set them beside her. She finished spreading butter and jam on the toast, and Dad grabbed the orange juice.

"Did you hear from Colin?" she asked softly when they sat down to eat at the breakfast counter.

"Yeah." Dad opened the ketchup and proceeded to drown his eggs. "Judge White is gone for the holidays, and they can't set bail until he gets back."

"Everyone will be here at one tomorrow. What time do I need to start the turkey?" Kaley bit a piece of bacon. As usual when Dad cooked it, the slices were perfectly crispy. She'd never hurt Mom's feelings, but floppy bacon made her want to gag.

"Maybe we should cancel—"

"No," Kaley said more sharply than she intended. "Look, the turkey's already thawed out. We have no idea how soon we'll be able to bail Mom out. Or if we can bail her out."

"This was a set-up," Dad snapped.

"And we're going to need to prove it," Kaley said calmly. "We need to find out what evidence the sheriff's department has." No matter how scared was, she needed to keep Dad from blowing up and doing something stupid—

"No," Dad said sharply. "Later tonight, we break her out of the county jail, Surely, there's a spell that could put the night shift to sleep—"

"No, Dad." Kaley shook her head. "We can't do that—"

"There's a town up in Montana that owes its allegiance to the St. James Coven." Dad waved in a westerly direction. "We can take her there—"

"No!" Kaley slammed her right palm on the countertop. "That's not going to work, Dad. Master St. James will be required to turn Mom over to Brown Dog if she's a fugitive, and if they find her guilty, they will kill her!" Kaley took Dad's hand in hers. "Our best bet is to find out who set Mom up."

"That's easy." Dad snorted, but he squeezed Kaley's hand back. "Humanity Now would love taking down a supernatural. Come to a small town where there's fewer supers in residence, and turn the Normals against the supers."

"That was definitely their plan." Kaley nibbled on her bacon. Something didn't feel right. "Did Mom leave the house last night after Kirsten and I hit the sack?"

Dad wouldn't meet her eyes. He stabbed at his eggs.

Her supper swirled with a nauseating certainty in her stomach. "Where did she go?"

Dad pushed back his plate. "She ran over to the *Monitor*. She said she forgot some paperwork."

"And no one went with her." So much for being hungry, but starving herself wasn't going to help anyone. Kaley ripped off a chunk of toast and popped it in her mouth. The blueberry jam and butter melting together in her mouth reminded her of her original question. "What time do I need to start the turkey?"

"Your mom got a twenty-five pounder—" Dad pulled out his phone and tapped it a few times. "Five to six hours, so . . ."

"I'll set my alarm for five," Kaley murmured. "I still need to deal with the giblets counting the prep time."

"We could get it ready tonight and stick it in the oven at seven," Dad said.

"I thought I was supposed to call Aunt Jo tonight." She shook her head. "I'll never get her off the phone before I pass out from exhaustion."

They both laughed, but it didn't alleviate the sick feeling in Kaley's stomach. Mom didn't have an alibi for last night, and she'd worked from home today. If their attorney and the rest of the family didn't figure out who killed Warren Simon, Mom was screwed.

Chapter 14 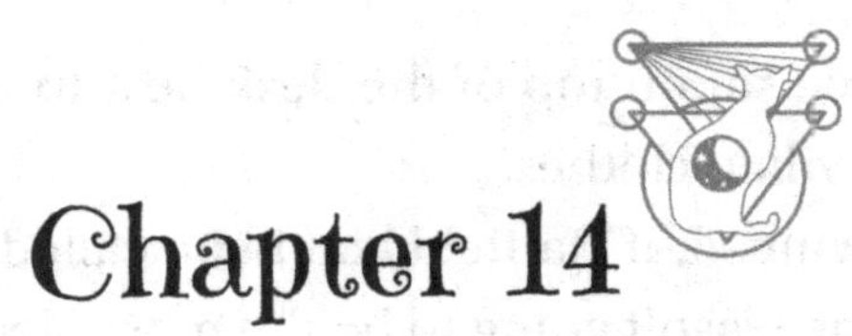

Kirsten stared at the vampire, not sure if he was joking until Jimmy said, "I'd be more worried about the garlic in the cheese balls they're having for tomorrow's appetizers if I were you." Both law officers started laughing.

Chief Enforcer Lambert looked at Kirsten and rolled her eyes. *Men.*

Despite the already very long day Kirsten had, she giggled at the other witch's comment.

"Can we get this started?" Donny said. "Some of us haven't had much sleep for the past forty-eight hours."

"Too much partying, little 'coyote," Robbins teased.

"Dude, I've got nothing to prove to you." Donny cocked his head to face the vampire who towered nearly a foot over him. "My best friend tripped over a dead body when all we were trying to do was get a blasted Christmas tree. Her mom's now been arrested for the murder. And to top off my week, I'm probably going to lose my college football scholarship. So, excuse me for not kissing your ring."

"Ignore him, Donny," Ellie said with a glare at Robbins. "He thinks he knows everything because he's married to his master."

"And you aren't afraid to sic your aunt or your great-grandfather on me," he responded. "Now, that we have that all settled, may we proceed to our actual business?"

"This way, folks." Jimmy motioned for them to follow him. The band of supernaturals and Family entered the administrative section of the building. Jimmy led them to the department's briefing room. Deputy Julia Wolford was passing out sets of papers on the tables facing the podium. Officer Mark Hatfield from the Millersburg Police sat on top of the desk next to the podium. He was dressed in civilian clothes.

Kirsten winced. If Hatfield had been called in when he had the holiday off, he wasn't going to be the most pleasant person to deal with during this investigation. That was assuming Jimmy would let her be involved.

It could have been worse. Hatfield's police partner Lewis Zarnecki was a member of Humanity Now.

Once the supernatural and Family guests were seated and had a copy of the sheriff's department report, Jimmy leaned his left elbow on the front of the podium and began.

"All right, everyone knows Warren Simon's body was discovered by the Wilson twins and Donny Fryer this afternoon around two-thirty at the Slaughters' Christmas tree farm. Magick was detected on his body. The Village of Millersburg and Holmes County are in the process of putting together a joint Normal and supernatural task force to deal with problems like this, but until it is formalized in January, your assistance has been requested since the victim is a member of Humanity Now."

"Excuse me, Sheriff." Officer Hatfield pointed at Kirsten. "Is having Kirsten here a good idea? Wasn't Rachel arrested for Simon's murder?"

"We can clear that up right now." Lambert turned in her chair to face Kirsten. "Ms. Wilson, did you kill Warren Simon?"

"No, ma'am."

"Do you know who did kill Warren Simon?"

"No ma'am."

Lambert looked at Tyler who was sitting in front of Kirsten. "Any change in her aura?"

He shook his head. "No, ma'am."

Lambert pivoted in her seat to look at Donny and Chief Enforcer Robbins. "Any change in her scent, gentlemen?"

They both shook their heads, though Robbins grinned, showing his very pointy canine teeth.

Lambert turned back to the sheriff and grinned. "I didn't See any change in her aura either. Your intern is clear, Jimmy, unless you want me to cast a Blood Oath on her."

He scowled at Officer Hatfield. "Any other objections before I continue, Mark?"

The Millersburg policeman jutted his chin in Ellie's direction. "Who's the dark-haired girl?"

Ellie jumped to her feet and stood at attention. "Enforcer Eleanor Howell of the St. James Vampire Coven. I'm accompanying Enforcer Levy-Fitzgerald."

Hatfield looked at her askance. "How old are you?"

"I'm seventeen," she said crisply.

"Officer Hatfield." Robbins addressed him in an amused tone. "Enforcer Howell has been trained by Ares of Olympus himself. Personally, I wouldn't question her capabilities."

The policeman stared at Ellie. "How, ur, why . . ."

"Short answer or long answer?" she asked.

"Short."

"He's my foster grandmother's dad, so he considers me one of his grandchildren," she stated. "And given my various relationships, he wanted to make sure I could defend myself as a Normal."

Officer Hatfield's mouth dropped open.

"As I was saying—" Sheriff Birkheimer paused to give Hatfield a dirty look. "Yes, Rachel has been arrested. She's got no alibi for the time the M.E.'s initial estimate of when Simon was probably killed. Again, that's why you're all here."

The senior enforcers exchanged confused looks.

"Why didn't you have Mr. Fryer in the interrogation room when Rachel Wilson was questioned?" Anne asked.

"Donny checking her scent isn't going to be acceptable evidence in a Normal court." Julia held up a hand. "No offense, Donny. My stepbrothers are werecoyotes."

"None taken," Donny said. He looked at Kirsten and tapped his temple.

What?

If she tells me that one more time, I'm going to chew up her favorite pair of boots.

She's trying to show she supports you.

I don't need her using me to prove she's not a bigot.

Then you need to pull up your big 'coyote panties, and tell her that.

Donny opened his mouth. Kirsten reached over and dug her fingernails into the thigh of his jeans and the flesh beneath. *Tell her privately after we're done here.*

"Telepathy won't be admissible either." Lambert raised her right eyebrow and stared at Kirsten and Donny.

"And it's not going to help us if we break Rachels's mind," Robbins added. "What about the fae that's living in Millersburg? Has anyone spoken with him?"

"Really?" Ellie said. "Why do you people go straight to blaming any fae around?"

"Don't you know your history, girl?" Robbins snapped. His eyes flamed from dark brown to glowing gold.

"Yeah, I do." Ellie shot him a vicious smile. "Like when your wife plotted to overthrow my uncle."

"Cut it out!" Jimmy knocked on the wooden podium. "We're supposed to be working together." He eyed Kirsten and Donny. "Did either of you talk to River after you left Jo's this afternoon?"

They looked at each other before Kirsten said, "No, but that doesn't mean Kaley didn't. They usually text each other before bed."

On the other side of Donny, Ellie snorted derisively. What was up her ass?

"We've got to check every possibility, Enforcer." Jimmy waved in the 'coyote's direction. "Donny smelled ozone on the corpse, but he couldn't pick up anything other than ozone and vestiges of Simon's Normal smell. No ginger. No honey."

"Then the corpse is the first thing we need to examine." Lambert waggled her right index finger to indicate herself and Tyler. They stood and moved toward the door.

Jimmy nodded. "Hatfield, take them over to the M.E.'s office. Chief Enforcer Lambert?"

She and Tyler paused.

"Please don't blow up the facility." He grinned. "We aren't the wealthiest county around, and we already lost one building and part of the high school grounds from magickal interaction this month. Even if River's not involved in this murder, we had a serial bomber sneak a few Unseelie charms into the county to make mixed magick explosive devices at the beginning of the month."

Lambert smiled and nodded. "Understood."

"John and I will check the site of the body dump," Anne said as she stood. "Ellie—"

"I got the records and research with Deputy Wolford and the Scooby gang." She jabbed her left thumb in Kirsten and Donny's direction. "We'll also track down River."

"I doubt if he was out of Cissy's sight once he got home yesterday," Julia murmured.

"We double-check everything," Jimmy said with a stern look at his deputy.

"Including the Humanity Now protesters?" Kirsten asked.

"That'll be my job," the sheriff assured her. "We need something solid because Rachel's fingerprints on Simon's wallet are damning as hell."

Kirsten's heart seemed to stop, and she couldn't catch her

breath. "What do you mean you found Mom's fingerprints on Simon's wallet?"

"That's the initial report." Jimmy's somber expression did nothing to reassure Kirsten. "Everything's being sent over to Columbus for confirmation."

"Okay." Kirsten nodded despite the thick nausea in her gut. They needed to find the murderer and fast. If Mom was tried by the Normal court system and lost, she was screwed. Ohio still had the death penalty for first degree murder.

Chapter 15 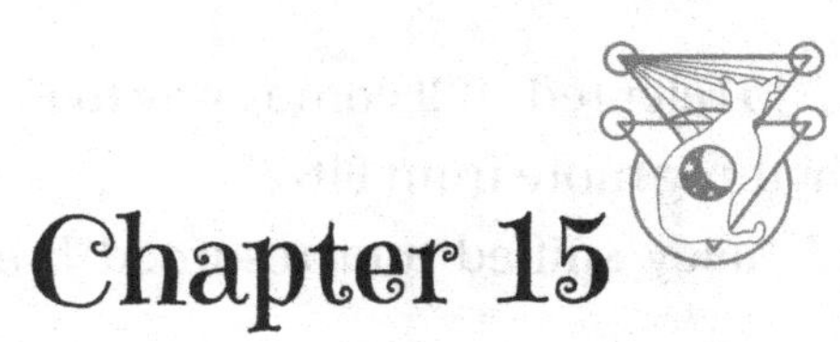

Kaley tapped the speed dial number for Jo and the speaker icon so she could break up the dried bread for tomorrow's dressing while they talked. She set her phone on the speaker stand while it rang.

"Kaley, are you all right?"

She smiled at the concern in Jo's voice. "I'm fine other than throwing up Mary's marvelous vegetable soup. I should have listened to Donny. He kept complaining he smelled something dead in the Slaughters' pine field." She retrieved a large mixing bowl and set it on the counter.

"I called the high priestess." The TV in the background at Jo's house went silent. "She's already dispatched our chief enforcer to Millersburg at Jimmy's request."

"Chief Enforcer Lambert arrived at the sheriff's department headquarters right before Dad and I left tonight." She broke bite-sized bits off of a piece of dried bread.

"What did she say?" Jo asked.

"She ordered Dad to take me and Kirsten home." Kaley grabbed the next slice and took out her frustrations on the innocent bread. The crunch satisfied some weird primal urge. "But Jimmy wanted Kirsten and Donny to stay a bit."

"Are you eating?" Jo asked. "I hear munching."

"Dad made me dinner. I'm breaking up the dried bread for tomorrow's dressing."

"Sweetheart, you don't have to—" Jo started.

"Yes, I do." Kaley swiped away her angry tears with the back of her hand. "We invited people over tomorrow, and we *will* deliver a Thanksgiving dinner."

"All right," Jo relented. "I'll come early to help. Have you or your dad heard anything more from Fitz?"

"Not yet." Kaley sniffed and resumed breaking up the dried bread.

"Call me when you do, and tell your dad the same," Jo ordered.

"Okay." Kaley said her goodbyes, but the instant she hung up, her phone rang again. River.

"Did you hear the news?" she asked.

"What news? Never mind. Open your bedroom window, but keep the lights off."

She wiped her hands on a dishtowel, picked up her phone, and turned off the speaker function.

Thank goodness, Dad was in the garage, using the shop vac to clean out all the dried mud she'd left behind. Even though Kirsten said she'd do it, Dad claimed he needed to keep busy.

"What's going on?" she asked breathlessly as she raced up the stairs.

"I'm being followed. I dropped Grandma off at Miz Rose's with instructions that they hightail it over to your Aunt Jo's place."

Kaley entered her bedroom. Green eyes from her bed reflected the hallway light. Penn gave a questioning meow.

"Where are you?" she said. A figure of shadow and ice crouched in the limbs of the ancient maple outside of her window. "Never mind."

She unlocked the window and shoved up the sash. A frigid wind gusted into her room. River threw a leg over the sill and crawled through the opening. As soon as he was upright, he slammed the sash shut, locked it, and pulled the blinds down.

"What's going on?"

"Remember that guy with Mrs. Ryder in the IGA parking lot?"

Kaley nodded.

"Sorry for not texting you back, but he's been following me

since yesterday." River closed the door to her bedroom. A thin sliver of light pierced the space between the bottom of the door and the hardwood floor. "When I heard on the radio your mom had been arrested, I was worried the Humanity Now idiots would come over here."

"Get in the hallway and sit down so they don't know you're here," Kaley commanded. "I need to call Kirsten and let her know what's happening. She's still at the sheriff's office. Let me make sure all the curtains and blinds are closed before you come downstairs."

She followed him out of her bedroom and shut the door behind them. River dropped to the floor while she thumbed the speed dial for her sister's number.

Footsteps stomped up the stairs. "Kaley, Teller's eating the bread—" Dad held Kirsten's cat, but his mouth dropped open when he saw River on the floor. Red flooded Dad's face. "How the hell did you get up here?" he roared.

Chapter 16

Kirsten blinked to clear her fuzzy vision as the three teenagers sat by themselves in the sheriff's briefing room. Everything from the walls and linoleum floor to the furniture were shades of brown and gray. The color scheme was soothing in a weird sort of way. Despite the ample number of colas Ellie generously provided, working at Jo's the last several days had taken its toll on Kirsten's cognitive abilities.

In the mush her brain had become, something in the reports didn't make sense. "I don't get how Mom could have touched Simon's wallet."

"What if she didn't think it was his?" Ellie said.

Both Kirsten and Donny stared at her.

"What if she were at the post office or bank or something?" Ellie waved her hand. "If the person in front of her dropped his wallet, what would she do?"

"Pick it up and give it back," Kirsten answered. "She hexed a lady's motor at Walmart's once to stop her long enough to return the purse she'd left in her cart."

"Would your mom do the same thing if it were Warren Simon?" Ellie persisted.

Kirsten shook her head. "Not after he pushed me on the street, and I nearly hit the asphalt face first."

"But why would whoever dumped Simon's body empty his wallet?" Donny asked.

"Make it look like Rachel was trying to pose the situation as a robbery gone wrong," Ellie said.

"So, it's plot within plot within a plot." He scratched his chin stubble that had gone way beyond five o'clock. "It sounds like something a fae would do."

Kirsten glared at him, as did Ellie.

He held up his hands. "I'm not saying it was any fae. But it sounds almost like the convoluted scheme River's mom put together to get revenge on his dad by bombing the town to start a race war."

"Is this Heather Martin?" Ellie asked. When both Kirsten and Donny nodded, Ellie continued, "From the reports I read, she's nuttier than a fruitcake."

"What reports?" Kirsten asked.

Ellie shrugged. "Anne's still technically a St. James enforcer. She had to write up a report for Grandpa Alex when Jo contacted her about the problems you were having a few weeks ago. And since she's my training officer, I'm supposed to review her reports and write up an analysis."

"Grandpa Alex?" Donny's eyebrows rose. "Is this another god?"

Ellie grinned. "Now, yeah. He's still the St. James chief enforcer."

"How many gods are in your family?" Kirsten asked.

Ellie sighed and gestured at the front of the room. "You do not have a white board big enough for my family tree. And if I tried, it's more convoluted than a telenovela."

"Back to our current problem." Kirsten tapped her stack of law enforcement reports. "We're also assuming the wallet found on the body was actually Simon's."

"His driver's license was in it," Ellie pointed out. "And the wallet has a lot of wear from the photos in our packets."

"This whole thing is getting way too complicated." Donny let his head drop, and his forehead gently hit the tabletop. A muffled "I'm too hungry and too tired to think anymore" filtered past his unruly hair and sweatshirt hood.

"It's got to be a Normal." Ellie tapped her own neon pink fingernails in a rapid rhythm. "Let's face it. If your mom had killed the guy, there's coven contingencies in place."

"What do you mean 'coven contingencies'?" Donny's head jerked up, and his attention flipped between Kirsten and Ellie.

The St. James enforcer stared at him in disbelief. "How does your pack deal with corpses?"

"He doesn't know what you're talking about because my family is the closest thing he has to pack," Kirsten said softly.

"Oh." Ellie frowned. "I apologize, Donny. I didn't realize your situation. What I mean is most of the covens and packs have access to an industrial incinerator to dispose of problems."

A horrified expression took over Donny's sharp features. "You just burn people to death you don't like?"

"No, they're mainly used to dispose of supernatural corpses." Ellie shook her head sadly. "With the recent advances in genetics, we can't take the chance of some idiot experimenting with supernatural DNA. Though there's been some cases where Normal Family members' bodies have to be cremated, like my dad."

"What the hell did your dad do?" Donny yelled.

"Chill, dude," Kirsten snapped.

"Dad didn't do anything wrong." Ellie swallowed hard. "His blood, and mine, are the basis for the V-virus vaccine and cure. When he died, my Family didn't want anyone to find out the Normal source for the cure. They also didn't want his remains to be used to create a bioweapon against the vampires who chose not to take the cure."

Donny eyed her. "But any super could take you!"

Kirsten groaned. Obviously, he hadn't listened when Robbins mentioned who had trained Ellie. Or maybe he thought Robbins was lying about gods on earth.

"Try it, dog-breath." Ellie lifted her chin in defiance.

Donny launched himself out of his chair, but for all his speed,

Ellie was already moving. He dove under the table. She rolled on top, reaching into her boot. When he came up on the other side, Ellie produced a large silver knife and brought the pommel down on the back of his neck. He howled in pain.

"What the hell is going on in here?" Julia hollered. The deputy stood in the doorway, her arms loaded with bags from one of the fast-food burger joints.

"Just proving a point," Ellie said with a smile. She sheathed her knife in her boot once again before she jumped down from the table and held out her palm to help Donny up off the floor.

Once he was upright, Ellie yanked the neckline of her black t-shirt back to show an ugly mass of scars at the join of her shoulder. "I guess Kaley didn't tell you, but a rogue vampire did this to me the day I turned four. The same one who beat the crap out of my dad and left him for dead. I had playdates with werewolves as a child. My foster grandmother is an Amazon. My foster grandfather was a Texas Ranger. And as Chief Enforcer Robbins pointed out I have more than one god for a relative. I've learned to survive."

She grabbed one of the bags Julia set on the table and tossed it to Donny. "Eat a couple of those. It'll speed up the healing of the silver burn on your neck."

When Donny dropped to his chair and unwrapped one of the cheeseburgers. Kirsten released the breath she'd held and turned to Julia. "Is Colin still here?"

The deputy nodded.

"Good. Ellie brought up a point we need to question Mom about."

Kirsten and Julia raced over to the interrogation room. Detective Mercer paced the hallway outside.

"Her attorney's still in there." He glared at Kirsten. "Or are you playing both sides?"

"Quit harassing the kid," Julia snapped before she knocked on the door and unlocked it.

Kirsten darted inside. Julia slammed the door shut behind her and locked it so the detective wouldn't follow. No doubt the deputy also stood guard as well.

Colin turned over his notepad. "Kirsten, you shouldn't be here."

Kirsten ignored him and turned to Mom. "Were you in any shops or other public places after the showdown in front of Jo's on Monday and when the rain started last night around five p.m.—"

"Don't answer that, Rachel," Colin snapped.

"Let me finish the question before you go constitutional on me, counselor," Kirsten bit back. "Mom, did someone drop a wallet that you picked up?"

The blood drained from her face. "Oh, Goddess! Yesterday, I ran by Mast Pharmacy to pick up a prescription for Miz Rose. The guy in front of me at the check-out counter dropped his wallet. He had a nasty scar on his face and more scars on his hand. He apologized and thanked me for handing him his wallet back. He said he had nerve damage from an accident years ago."

A shiver ran through Kirsten. "The scar on his face. Where was it?"

Mom drew her finger down her right cheek. Kirsten swallowed hard. That sounded exactly like the guy Kaley pointed out at the courthouse.

Chapter 17

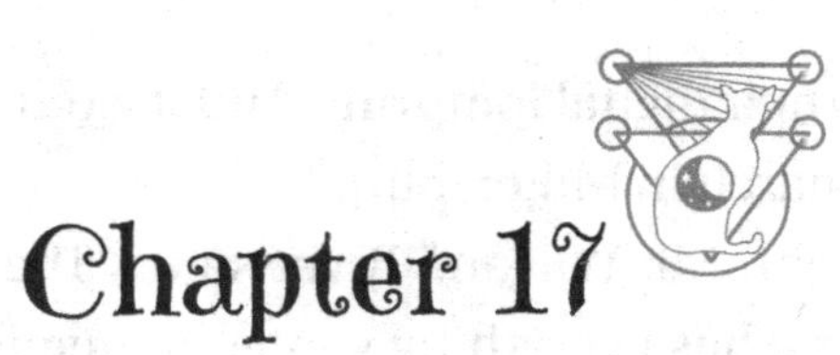

Kaley stepped between Dad and River. "Chill, Dad! He came here on foot because someone's following his car."

"He was in your room!" Dad roared.

Teller meowed loudly.

Behind Kaley, River's tennies squeaked on the hardwood, and his body heat radiated against her back. She did her best to ignore him and focused on the more immediate situation.

"Dad, you're hurting Teller. Please put him down."

He carefully placed Kirsten's cat on the floor. Teller lowered his ears and hissed at Dad before the gray tabby flicked his tail defiantly and stalked into Kirsten's bedroom.

"River climbed up the maple so none of the neighbors would see him," Kaley added calmly.

"You are not helping your cause, young lady," Dad growled.

"Dr. Wilson, the guy tailing me was with Mrs. Ryder at the grocery store on Monday when she was harassing Kaley," River said. "I think he may be with Humanity Now. He's been following me all day. To Jo's coffee shop, back to Grandma's, and the rest of the afternoon while I drove her on her errands after she closed the beauty shop early. I took her to Miz Rose's house about a half hour ago, and I told them to drive straight to Jo's while I walked here. Call Jo if you don't believe me."

"Why would he follow you?" Dad was still angry, but his fury was dying under hers and River's logic.

"What if Kirsten's right, and Humanity Now discovered River and his teacher back in Indianapolis are supernatural?" Kirsten said. "These days, it's not hard to find someone if they haven't totally erased their digital footprint. And it would explain why they've decided to march in Millersburg."

"She's right, Mr. Wilson," River said. "The high school administration alone has everything someone needs to identify me. And with my grandmother applying to be my legal guardian, my case is a matter of public record. I came here hoping maybe you and Mrs. Wilson could help me."

"Help you?" Dad stared at River. "We kind of have a crisis of our own—"

"Dad, be nice," Kaley warned. "He doesn't know, and you charged up here before I could tell him." She turned to River. "I tripped over Warren Simon's body when we went to get our Christmas tree out at the Slaughter's farm this afternoon. Mom's been arrested for his murder."

"Oh, crap." River raked his hands through his spikey white hair. "When did this happen?"

"She discovered the corpse almost seven hours ago," Dad said. "I'm sorry for losing my temper with you."

"If some idiot climbed into my daughter's window, I'd probably have the same reaction," River admitted. "But I'm serious about needing help. I've already lost my mother. I can't lose Grandma Cissy, too."

Dad nodded. "Any chance either of you got a photo of this guy?"

Kaley flipped through her phone to the picture River had her take of the man in the IGA parking lot. "This is him. Both Kirsten and I spotted him watching all of us as we left the coffee shop yesterday, but we didn't see him today." She handed her phone to Dad before she looked at River.

"I am so sorry he followed you," she said. "He was eyeing me and Kirsten, so she dodged through alleys for a bit yesterday to make sure he didn't tail us. We didn't think you and Donny were equally in danger with Humanity Now focused on Aunt Jo's café."

Dad handed back her phone. "Text me the picture, and text it to your sister and Donny, too. I'll send it to Jimmy and Jo. You'd both better come downstairs."

Kaley opened her mouth, but Dad raised his hands. "I'm more worried about the cats eating our Thanksgiving dinner and puking in your beds. River, you're more than welcome to stay here tonight. I'll make sure Cissy knows you're safe."

River nodded. "Thanks, Doctor Wilson."

Dad narrowed his eyes. "Just remember what I said about steers."

"I remember." River's expression remained solemn, but there was a slight twinkle in his eyes. "I don't want to end up on the wrong end of a steel knife. Or a scalpel."

After Kaley texted the picture of River's stalker along with River's recent experience to Kirsten and Donny, she helped Dad close all the blinds and curtains on the first floor. When she yelled up they were finished, River came downstairs to the kitchen. Both cats rubbed against his legs and purred.

Dad sighed. "Congratulations, River. You've been accepted into the glaring."

"Wait a minute." Kaley propped her fists on her hips. "Why do Teller and Penn's opinions carry more weight than mine or Kirsten's?"

"Because comparatively, the cats are older than you and your sister," Dad teased. His phone rang before Kaley could reply. "Hey, Jimmy!" He stepped into the dining room and closed the French doors.

Kaley couldn't help rolling her eyes. In a little over nine months, she and her twin would be eighteen. Would Dad and Mom even acknowledge she and Kisten were legal adults next Thanksgiving?

River looked inside the bowl still sitting on the counter. "Why were you breaking up dried-out bread?"

Kaley frowned. "Haven't you ever had homemade dressing before?"

He shook his head. "With Mom's work schedule, she'd roast a turkey breast and make the instant stuffing in a saucepan." He grinned. "I was actually looking forward to an old-fashioned Thanksgiving dinner."

"Part of the deliciousness is the work." She grinned back. "Time to contribute."

"But Grandma Cissy is bringing the sweet potatoes . . ." He closed his eyes and shook his head. "I actually forgot about the stuff with Humanity Now for a couple of minutes."

"That's probably a good thing," Kaley said. "I'm trying to wear myself out so I don't have nightmares about tripping over a dead man this afternoon."

"I'm sorry you had to deal with that." He stepped closer to her.

For a split second, it seemed as if he would kiss her. Instead, he grabbed the bowl and the plastic bag with the rest of the dried-out bread.

"I think I can handle breaking up crunchy bread." He smiled a sweet smile that made her toes melt into the sheepskin interior of her leather slippers.

"Th-thanks." She swallowed hard. "I'll mix up the pie dough and pumpkin while you do that.

Kaley busied herself with cutting the dough and rolling it out while River finished breaking up the bread crumbs. She had him dice the onion and celery for the dressing while she blended the pumpkin, milk, eggs, and spices together for the pie filling. By the time, she carefully placed the two glass pie plates into the oven and shut the door, he had dumped the chopped veggies into a medium-sized plastic bowl. She handed him the appropriate lid to seal it, and he popped them into the refrigerator for tomorrow.

"Now what?" he asked as he rinsed off the knife and cutting board.

Before Kaley could answer, someone pounded on the front door. Fear shot through her, pricking her flesh with its intensity. River followed her into the living room, only to find Dad answering the door.

Uncle Jimmy stepped inside, still in his official uniform. "We got him."

"Who?" Kaley asked.

"The guy that's been tailing River today." Jimmy grinned. "Nice job with the photo. Are you trying to compete with Kirsten for the internship?"

Kaley shook her head. "No, and the photo was River's idea after Mrs. Ryder's screaming fit at the grocery store on Monday."

"Where's Kirsten?" Dad asked.

"She drove Donny back to the coffee shop to pick up his car." Jimmy took off his hat. "I'm sorry Rachel is stuck in the jail for the holiday weekend. But I promise the entire staff will keep an eye on her. If you want to take some of your Thanksgiving dinner down to her tomorrow afternoon, it won't be a problem."

"Thanks, Jimmy," Dad said. "What about Rose and Cissy?"

"They're staying at Jo's for tonight."

"Did I make a stupid decision?" River blurted. "If the idiots from Humanity Now go after Jo, my grandmother will be in the line of fire."

Kaley laid her hand on his arm. "Actually, you made the right decision. Jo's house is the safest place in town."

River shook his head. "I respect her abilities, but she's only one person."

"She has help." Kaley sucked in a deep breath. "She'll ask the ghosts to keep watch."

"Ghosts?" Both of River's eyebrows rose.

"There's quite a few who reside in various places in town." Kaley shrugged. "Jo lives in one of the oldest houses in Millersburg, so she has a few ghosts."

River's disbelief plucked at Kaley's nerves. "Does Grandma Cissy know about them?"

"Pretty much everybody in town knows which places are haunted," Kaley said. "It's not really a big deal."

Jimmy chuckled. "Take him over to the Millersburg Hotel or the Victorian House Museum sometime." He turned back to Dad. "I work noon to eight tomorrow. Give me a call before you come over to the jail."

"Aren't you going to have Thanksgiving with Finlay?" Dad asked.

Who's Finlay? River asked silently.

Jimmy's girlfriend, Kaley answered. *She has a craft shop in Berlin.*

"We're celebrating on Monday when her store's closed." Jimmy placed his hat on his head. "Try to get some sleep, man." He eyed Kaley and River. "That goes for you kids, too." He opened the door.

Kirsten stood on the porch, in the middle of reaching for the door latch.

"Hey, Jimmy." She entered the house.

"Have a good night." He nodded to Kirsten and pulled the door shut behind him as he left.

"What were you doing for the last couple of hours?" Dad asked.

"Combing through the evidence and reports collected so far." She shook her head. "We're pretty sure Mrs. Ryder's buddy from the IGA is the one who set Mom up, but the prosecutor wants to question him before he will release Mom. And of course, everyone's gone for the holiday weekend."

"Crap." Dad rubbed the back of his neck. "I know everyone's doing their job, but the timing sucks."

"Is there ever a good time to be accused of a crime?" River asked sourly.

Kaley winced. Time to change the subject before everyone wallowed in their bad luck. "Kirsten, did Donny get home all right?"

Her twin's phone buzzed. She pulled it out of her pocket and checked the text. "Yes, he did. He and his mom will be here at eleven to help with dinner." Kirsten tapped out an answer to Donny.

Kaley ticked off on her fingers the prep work she and River had completed. "The pumpkin pies are in the oven. The bread's broken up, and the onions and celery are chopped for the dressing—"

Glass from the front window exploded through the curtains with a loud crash, and shards landed all over the couch.

Chapter 18

Kirsten cursed as a brick tore the curtains, bounced off the couch and landed on the area rug. Bits of glass tinkled as they hit the bare hardwood plank flooring behind the couch. Outside, an engine roared. Dad raced to the front door. She ran after him, but by the time she reached the porch, Dad was running down the sidewalk. Tires screeched. She only caught a glimpse of tail lights as the vehicle veered left onto the side street.

Dad jogged back to the house from the direction the vandals had disappeared. Waves of fury emanated from him. "They had to have been waiting for Jimmy to leave."

"Did you get a good look at the car?" she asked.

"Yeah, and a partial plate." He took the steps two at a time and paused at the sight of the window. "What are these idiots doing? Trying to relive Kristallnacht?"

Kirsten couldn't breathe. The heat of his rage smothered her.

Dad charged into the house. Kirsten followed him once again. The temperature in the living room had noticeably dropped with the giant hole in the front window. Kaley held the brick, staring at it like it was a rattlesnake.

"You two, okay?" he asked Kaley and River.

"We're fine." River scowled. "But you should see this, Doctor Wilson." He pointed at the brick.

Dad walked over to Kaley. Kirsten joined him and read the message on the brick in black permanent marker from the odor.

You will all burn, bitches.

"Well, that's a warm and friendly Thanksgiving note," Kirsten commented.

"Why didn't your warding work?" River asked.

"Passive warding can't stop physical objects from outside of the protected area," Kirsten said. "And whoever threw the brick did it from the street, not on our lot."

"Could River's portal from three weeks ago have interrupted your mother's wards?" Dad held up his hands before Kaley could launch into one of her tirades about witch bigotry. "I'm not accusing anyone of anything. If the witch and fae magicks mess up each other, could they have—"

"It's totally possible, sir." River wore a dejected expression. "I'm sorry. I barely understand my own abilities, but I never intended to put you and your family in danger."

Dad laid a hand on River's shoulder. "I know you didn't, and I'm not blaming you."

Kirsten glanced at Kaley, but her twin said nothing, aloud or silently. But the expression on her sister's face said volumes. Kaley knew River had saved her a second time by opening a portal to Otherwhere and sending the bullet from his mom's handgun into the space between dimensions. Poor River didn't even understand what he'd done at first.

"Let me call Jimmy, and get him back over here," Dad said. "Girls, don't try to clean up anything until we take some pictures. River, there's some plywood stacked in the garage on the side closest to the house. Would you grab a sheet and set it on the front porch? I'll grab my toolbox and meet you out there in a minute."

"But what about someone seeing River here?" Kaley protested.

"That brick could be a warning after the police nabbed the jerk following River," Kirsten said. "It doesn't matter if we shield River because every supernatural in town is a target."

"We can theorize all we want," Dad said. "But we need to collect the evidence to prove anything. Kaley, honey, can you please stop contaminating every crime scene?"

She carefully set the brick on the rug while Dad stalked back to the kitchen, pulling his phone from his jeans pocket as he walked.

Kirsten hugged herself against the cold air swirling through the giant hole in the glass. Dad was right. She was jumping to conclusions. The brick may not have anything to do with the guy following River. Or everything tonight could be an orchestrated effort to harass the supernaturals living in town.

Which meant the news had already leaked that magick had been detected on Warren Simon's body.

Uncle Jimmy pulled up in front of the house five minutes after Dad called him. He jumped out of his SUV and strode up to the porch. Dad and River held the plywood in place while Kirsten and Mr. Gregory from across the street finished nailing the piece to the window frame. Inside, Kaley had nailed up an ancient quilt for some insulation.

Jimmy jogged up the porch steps. "Everyone okay here, Ethan?"

"Yeah." He paused long enough for Kirsten to drive in the last nail. "Luckily, no one was sitting on the couch when the brick flew through the window."

"Pat Hall pulled Colton Harper over for speeding," Jimmy said without any preamble. "Josh Fairbanks was in the car with him. His plate matches the first half of the tag number you were able to see."

Kirsten suppressed the shiver in her spine. "Tan Corolla?"

"According to the chief," Jimmy said.

"That's the car all right," Dad said sourly.

"You want to press charges, Ethan?" Jimmy asked.

"In my day, I would have gotten an ass-whooping from my father for pulling something like this," Mr. Gregory commented. "And that was after Sheriff Hindle threw the book at me."

"Sounds like there's a story." Jimmy chuckled.

"Another time." Mr. Gregory grinned. "Don't want to corrupt Doc Wilson's girls with my boyhood antics."

Kirsten held her breath, hoping Dad would do the right thing. Except she was no longer sure what the right thing was.

"Nah, I think I'll do something worse." Dad's grin scared her. "I'm going to call their parents."

Chapter 19

Fifteen minutes later, Kaley could barely believe it when Police Chief Hall escorted Josh and Colton into the Wilsons' house. Dad and Jimmy had to be out of their minds. The chief wasn't looking too happy about this plan either.

What was even worse, Josh wouldn't even look at Kaley where she sat in one of the plush armchairs. She'd ended things with him before they really started a romantic relationship. Partly out of guilt over him being targeted because of Heather Martin's desire for revenge. Partly because she had feelings for River. In fact, Josh almost felt guilty himself.

However, she didn't need to be a witch to read Colton. He glared at everyone with cold rage.

"Sit down, gentlemen." Dad patted the backs of the two dining room chairs he'd carried into the living room before the chief and her detainees arrived.

When the two boys hesitated, Chief Hall said, "You can sit down, or the sheriff and I take you to jail."

Josh and Colton looked at each other before they crossed to the chairs and sat down on them.

Shaking, Kaley rose from the armchair and approached Josh. "Did you throw the brick through our window because I said we should just be friends?"

"No." Josh brushed aside the thick shock of hair that always seemed to be in his eyes.

"Then why did you call me and my sister bitches?" Her eyes burned. She felt so guilty even though she did nothing to cause his magickal injuries near the beginning of the month.

No words. No excuses. Not even an apology. He stared at the tips of his tennies.

The silence was broken by a brusque knock on the front door.

"Kirsten, who's on the porch?" Dad said.

Air froze in Kaley's lungs. What was Dad trying to prove by making Kirsten use her abilities in front of Josh and Colton?

"It's Mr. and Mrs. Fairbanks and Mr. Harper," Kirsten said quietly.

Dad shook his head and glared at the boys. "Did you really think you were going to get away with throwing a brick through my window?"

He crossed to the door as the second knock rattled the heavy wood. When he opened it, Mrs. Fairbanks charged inside and yelled, "What do you think you are doing, Ethan Wilson? So help me—"

"Shut up, Lainie," Mr. Fairbanks snapped as he followed his wife into the house. "You're making things worse."

Mr. Harper stepped inside, wearing a sad and weary expression. Life hadn't given him a fair shake, and it showed in the deep lines on his face. They made him look way more than three years older than Dad.

Dad shook the two men's hands. "I apologize for the late calls the night before Thanksgiving." Mrs. Fairbanks ignored Dad, so he didn't even try to shake her hand.

"Here's the deal, folks," Chief Hall said brusquely. "Doctor Wilson has agreed to forgo charges against Josh and Colton for vandalism and assault if the following conditions are met. One, the boys pay for the window out of their own pockets. No money from the parents. If they cannot produce the funds on Friday, they will work off their debt at the vet clinic over Christmas break since his staff would love to take some time off with their families."

Kaley bit her tongue to keep a nervous giggle from escaping at the astonished look on Mrs. Fairbanks's face.

"Two, Colton and Josh will steer clear of the Wilson girls at school, and vice versa. That includes any of their friends," Chief Hall continued. "Finally, Kirsten will no longer provide any tutoring to the boys. You need to find someone else."

"Before you make any decisions, folks," Jimmy drawled. "The boys are also looking at attempted murder and terroristic threats with a healthy side of hate crimes, which are all felonies. But even with this incident knocked down to the initial charges Chief Hall presented, they can and probably will be charged as adults."

"Judge White will—" Mrs. Fairbanks started.

"Throw our son into jail," Mr. Fairbanks said. "You're the one who donated to his campaign because of his tough-on-crime platform."

"And with a criminal record, the boys will probably lose all of their potential football scholarships," Dad added.

"I can't believe this!" Mrs. Fairbanks shrieked. "Your wife's a murderer, and you're threatening my son!"

Dad stiffened at her accusations, but he pursed his lips and kept silent.

Funny how Josh's mom was starting to sound exactly like Amelia's mom. Kaley's eyes burned, and she clenched her fists to keep from stalking over to Mrs. Fairbanks and decking her. If she did that, she was as stupid and mean as Amelia, Colton, and Josh. And not pursuing her initial crush with Josh was looking more and more like a blessing.

"Fine." Chief Hall shrugged. "Then the boys go to jail. You won't be able to make bail until Judge White gets home from his in-laws on Monday."

"May I say something first?" Mr. Harper's quiet words grabbed everyone's attention. He rarely smiled, much less showed any other emotion, but an ache showed on his face.

Chief Hall nodded. "Go ahead, Ray."

"I don't mean to step on your toes, Doc, but you're being too kind to my son." Mr. Harper stared at Colton. Waves of disappointment rolled off both him and Mr. Fairbanks compared to Mrs. Fairbanks's fury.

Mr. Harper took a deep breath before he continued. "You could have killed someone, Colton. What if one of the twins' friends or family were sitting there when that brick came through the window? Didn't you learn anything over your mother's death? Grant Carter was just hunting at his place when his bullet ricocheted and hit your mother. It was an accident, but poor Grant is still sitting in Marion Correctional for being drunk and careless. I just want to know why you did this."

"I don't know," Colton murmured. "It just wasn't fair Kaley survived an explosion, and Mom died."

Kaley exchanged looks with her twin. Kirsten looked as guilty as Kaley felt. If it weren't for River healing her, she'd still be in a sling for her broken shoulder blade after the explosion at the Painter Building.

Or dead.

"That's life, son." Mr. Harper shook his head. "Nothing's fair for anybody, but your mother taught you better. What did she tell you when you tried to bully little Donny Fryer because his own daddy was dead?"

"Life's hard enough without me being cruel to those less fortunate," Colton choked out.

Josh leapt to his feet. "Nothing bad happened in this town until Kaley and Kirsten showed off their powers in front of everyone."

"That's not true, and you know it, Fairbanks."

Kaley jumped along with everyone else in the room. River released the shadows of the staircase and came down the rest of the way, Teller and Penn at his heels. He was supposed to be in the guest room, but he must have decided he was going to participate in this situation against Dad's advice.

"My mom was raped in this town, and my grandmother threw Mom out of her house because she got pregnant," River stated. "It drove her crazy, and now, she's in a psych ward. And that all started nine months before I was born, so don't you *dare* tell me this bull-crap started last month!"

Josh blinked and swallowed hard as River strode up to him.

"As a little reminder, my mother, a Normal, is the one who hurt you, not any supernatural," River continued. "And it was a supernatural who healed you in the hospital."

Josh's face turned pasty white at the same time Mrs. Fairbanks' cheeks blushed a brilliant red.

"What's he talking about, Josh?" Mr. Fairbanks asked.

When Josh didn't answer, his mom stepped toward him with an expression of sheer disbelief. "What are you hiding from us?"

"Donny came to visit me at the hospital." Josh swallowed hard. "He said the doctors weren't telling us the truth. That I was dying. Then he asked if I trusted him. When I said yes, he left and came back with him." Joshua jutted his chin in River's direction. "The new kid. Miz Cissy's grandson."

Kaley trembled. As far as she knew, Kirsten and Donny were the only others besides her who knew what River had done for Josh. But the guys hadn't told her and Kirsten the truth either. Oh, Goddess! This was going to blow up in their faces.

"You laid a spell on my son?" Mrs. Fairbanks hissed at River.

"No, he didn't," Kaley said. "Healing is a totally different technique than spellcasting, And it's a very rare talent among both fae and witches."

"Like I said, it was my mother's fault both Kaley and Josh were hurt," River said. "I did what I could to fix the situation."

"No one's perfect, Mrs. Fairbanks," Kirsten said. "The ER docs missed a bleed in Kaley's brain when the explosion at the Painter Building threw her into the concrete wall of the auto supply shop."

"And Josh was poisoned by whatever Heather Martin used to keep her bombs from going off prematurely," Kaley added.

"Has Chief Enforcer Lambert told you something she hasn't told Pat and me?" Jimmy eyed the girls.

"No," Dad replied. "But in the interest of full disclosure, I think the Fairbanks have a right to know that Brown Dog and Dare Covens did a thorough investigation in conjunction with you and Chief Hall over Heather Martin's actions. And the covens' enforcers are assisting your inquiry into Warren Simon's death. No one, Normal or supernatural, is taking what happened to Josh or Simon lightly." He shot River a pointed look. "But it would have been nice if you'd told Chief Hall or Sheriff Birkheimer what you'd done for Josh."

"That was my fault," Kaley stepped between her dad and her friend. "With everyone freaking out about River moving to Millersburg, I told him not to say anything."

"Why would people being upset about River living here?" Mr. Harper asked.

Jimmy cleared his throat. "Remember the murders and animal mutilations about seventeen years ago?"

Mr. Harper nodded along with the Fairbanks.

"A fae noble started all the trouble in order to score political points with his queen," Jimmy said. "He was caught, and in the aftermath, Colin Fitzgerald negotiated that the noble's people could leave in peace on the condition no fae from either court steps foot in Holmes County ever again."

"Fae quite literally cannot break a promise," Kaley said. "And that's the only point where Mr. Fitzgerald screwed up in his negotiations. He should have said anyone with fae blood. Technically, River is only half-fae, and as such, he doesn't belong to either court." She shrugged. "Therefore, he can live in Holmes County. But everyone who knew about the deal initially freaked out when the Martins moved back to Millersburg." She glared at Uncle Jimmy.

Mr. Harper looked at Colton. "My grandfather fought the Nazis to keep them from killing everyone who they deemed unworthy. Why on earth would you join a bunch of people who believe murder is okay?"

Colton broke under his father's aching sadness. He choked back a sob before he whispered, "I'm sorry, Dad."

"I'm not the one you owe an apology to," Mr. Harper murmured.

"Why don't you and Colton come over for Thanksgiving dinner tomorrow?" Dad turned to Kaley. "We're still shooting for one p.m., aren't we?"

She nodded, a little unsure about the sudden change of this entire encounter.

Go with it, her twin whispered in her mind.

Fine, she would. "Mr. and Mrs. Fairbanks, you and Josh are welcome to join us, too."

"I'm not—" Mrs. Fairbanks started.

"We'd be delighted, Kaley," Mr. Fairbanks said. "We'll bring seven-layer salad and apple pie. It smells like you have the pumpkin pies covered." He grinned.

"You can't—" Mrs. Fairbanks tried again.

"We were going to do a single turkey breast," Mr. Harper said. "I can cook that and the potatoes ahead of time, and mash the taters when we arrive."

"That would be wonderful." Kaley smiled at Mr. Harper before she turned to Josh. "Will you please tell me why you are so angry with me?"

"I thought you liked me," he muttered.

"I did, um, do." She swallowed and tried to grasp her thoughts amid the tide of her emotions. "I felt guilty about what happened to you. Ms. Martin was trying to harm me and you because . . ."

"Because of the fae guy and what he did to her—" Josh shuffled his feet like he was suddenly aware the adults were staring at the two of them.

"Yes, and I felt responsible because she dragged you into her convoluted plan."

"And I can't compete against River," Josh muttered.

"What makes you think—" she started.

"When he healed me, I suddenly knew how he felt about you." Josh brushed his hair out of his eyes again. "And he's supernatural, and I'm not."

"Except it's not up to you guys to decide who my sister likes," Kirsten snapped. "So, if that brick was some jealousy crap, it needs to stop now."

"You changing your terms, Ethan?" Jimmy asked.

Dad shook his head. "I think my terms are more than fair."

"I agree with Ray," Mr. Fairbanks said. "Let's add on weekends from now until the end of the school's winter break for the boys' service at your clinic. If you don't mind, he and I will pay for the window so it's replaced on Friday. No sense in your girls freezing over the holiday weekend because our sons did something stupid and dangerous."

"All right." Dad nodded.

"One last thing, Doctor Wilson. You will call me or Sheriff Birkheimer if Josh or Colton fail to show up at the clinic." Chief Hall didn't even make it a question.

"Yes, ma'am." Dad maintained his serious façade, but his humor was returning, which was a bit of a relief.

Mrs. Fairbanks still argued with her husband, albeit under her breath, as the Fairbanks and the Harpers left the house.

Dad broke the quiet. "So, anything new in the investigation of Simon's death?"

Chapter 20

Kirsten wanted to drop through the floor. Dad's attempt at humor was not only embarrassing, but in poor taste in front of her potential employers. Not to mention, the timing of his question could have been better.

"Thanks to Kirsten, Donny, and Ellie, Jimmy and I have to get back to the sheriff's department." Chief Hall grinned. "I'm looking forward to watching Chief Enforcer Robbins interrogating River's stalker." She immediately sobered. "But we need to be realistic and logical. Follow the evidence and make our case."

"Don't worry, Ethan." Jimmy clapped Dad's shoulder. "Fitz will make sure we do everything by the book in regards to Rachel."

Once the law officials said their goodbyes and left the house, Dad turned to Kirsten. "Please tell me they were telling me the truth."

Kirsten had always viewed Dad as the rock of the family. It was unsettling for him to ask her for reassurance. She nodded. "Chief Hall wasn't lying about her enjoyment at siccing Dare's chief enforcer on a Humanity Now member."

"Neither the chief or Sheriff Birkheimer think Mrs. Wilson is guilty," River added. "They're worried about finding whoever did kill Simon."

"What about Robbins butting heads with Fitz, Anne, and the enforcer who accompanied them?" Dad asked.

"It hasn't really happened." Kirsten shook her head. "And I don't think it will. Chief Enforcer Robbins and Ellie did the typical one-upmanship that goes with being members of different vampire covens, but they're both taking their cues from Uncle Jimmy and immediately got to work tonight."

"Ouch." Kaley winced. "I hope Chief Hall isn't taking their deference to Jimmy personally."

Kirsten shook her head again. "She isn't. She knows he's worked with supernaturals before, and Anne and Robbins in particular. It's part of the reason she broached the subject of the joint taskforce with him. He's got more personal contacts than she does." She shrugged. "But they both need to adhere to Normal laws since the victim is a Normal and the crime happened in their jurisdiction."

"But what about—" Dad started.

"Stop." Kirsten held up her hands. "Mom's okay. The Holmes County Jail doesn't keep their prisoners in silver, spell-threaded manacles. On the off-chance Officer Zarnecki or some other member of Humanity Now tries to hurt her while she's in her cell, she can defend herself. But we three—" She gestured at herself, Kaley, and River. "—have been up since four this morning. If we're cooking tomorrow, we need some sleep."

Kaley crossed her arms and scowled. "And unless you plan on making River sleep in the garage, we need to get him towels and a toothbrush."

Dad's face turned beet red, and a mix of irritation and embarrassment emanated from him. "He can stay in the guest room, but he'd better behave."

"I will, Doctor Wilson." River grinned. "I'd rather eat a steer than be one."

The next morning, River's assistance came in handy while Kirsten and Kaley prepped for Thanksgiving dinner. He helped Kaley wash the dust off of Grandma Charlie's wedding china. Kirsten was putting together the green bean casserole while the giblets simmered in a saucepan when her phone rang.

"It's probably Donny saying his mom needs some more sleep, and they'll be late," she joked, but it was Chief Hall's number on the screen. She thumbed the answer icon. "Hey, Chief! Are you joining us for Thanksgiving dinner at one?"

"No, but I am calling to ask you to come down to the jail," the chief said.

Alarm crashed through her and ricocheted off Kaley's psyche. "Is Mom okay?"

"Your mother is fine," Chief Hall reassured her. "John Robbins guarded her through the night. He's requested you and Donny to be here when we question Burt Stedman instead of him."

"Burt Stedman?" Kirsten glanced at Kaley and River, but they felt as confused as she did. They listened to the chief's end of the conversation through Kirsten. She clamped down on the urge to slap at the mental itch River's fae magick produced.

"The guy we picked up for stalking River," the chief explained. "We ran a background check, and Ellie Howell confirmed the information through her own—methods. This morning, your mother visually identified him as the man at the pharmacy in front of her who dropped the wallet her fingerprints were found on."

"I thought you and Chief Enforcer Robbins were going to question him last night."

"Anne suggested letting Stedman see John vamped out then allow him to stew in a cell overnight. Since your mom was already asleep and Stedman didn't demand an attorney last night, I agreed."

"But why do you need us?" Kirsten flipped off the burner for the giblets.

"John has a plan, but he had to leave before dawn." Chief Hall paused. "I can't tell you more over the phone." She sighed. "This is one time I had wished I telepathy like you. I could tell you without anyone overhearing."

Kirsten laughed. "It's not that simple."

"That's what Jill and John said." Chief Hall chuckled. "How soon can you get here?"

"Give me twenty minutes." Kirsten tapped the icon to end the call. "Can you two handle things until Jo arrives?"

Kaley smirked. "Do we have a choice?"

"Do not wake up Dad," Kirsten warned.

Kaley rolled her eyes. "I'm not that evil. I heard him pacing around down here last night, too." Her attitude washed away with a glimmer of tears. "Tell Mom we love her if you have a chance."

Kirsten nodded and swallowed hard. "I will—" Her phone chimed with an incoming text. "Now what?" she said through clenched teeth as she thumbed the app icon.

"Well?" River asked as she read the message.

"Donny's mom." Kirsten tapped a reply and slipped her phone back in her jeans pocket. "They're almost here. She says she'll help you while Donny and I head over to the jail." She looked up.

River's hands rested on her twin's shoulders. Kirsten could feel him radiating his strength through Kaley. Maybe things were a lot more serious between them than she realized.

She glanced at the time on the microwave before she fetched her coat from its peg. "We'll try to be back before one."

"Don't sweat it," Kaley replied. "I promise to save some dressing and pumpkin pie for you. It's more important to find out how this Stedman is connected to Simon's death."

Kirsten nodded before she headed for the front door. Part of her hoped this guy was connected to the body her sister tripped over. Otherwise, they were back to square one.

Chapter 21

Kaley discovered organizing a holiday dinner was a lot like organizing a prom. Somebody had to keep all the volunteers focused on their tasks. It was a little weird that even the adults listened to her, but then, she was the only Wilson present and awake who knew where everything was in the kitchen cabinets.

Jo brought parmesan and red pepper egg bites as well as a selection of pastries for everyone to nibble on while they worked. She ironed the marigold-colored cloth napkins before she tucked Miz Rose in an out-of-way spot. The elderly Normal folded the napkins into turkey shapes.

As he promised, Mr. Harper brought boiled potatoes, but the huge pot had to have contained five pounds of spuds. He'd also cooked and pre-sliced the roasted turkey breast he and Colton brought.

When Kaley caught Colton feeding bits of turkey to Teller and Penn, he blushed before he asked to speak to her privately. They went into the mudroom, and he closed the door.

"I apologize for the stupid stuff I did last night." He shuffled his feet and wouldn't meet her eyes. "It wasn't just my mom's death I was upset about. Josh lied to me about what really happened between you, him, and River. I shouldn't have assumed you would lead him on only to stomp on his feelings."

Kaley snorted. "You wouldn't be the first guy who chose bros before hoes."

Colton's cheeks turned from pink to red. "You're not a hoe, Kaley."

"No, I'm not." She Looked at his aura. Colton definitely regretted his actions from last night. Still, she needed to make things crystal clear between them, "But in the future, please make sure you know both sides before throwing bricks."

"I will." He nodded, though he still wouldn't look at her.

Well, if she had acted like a jerk, maybe she'd be just as embarrassed, too.

Kaley and Colton returned the kitchen at the same time Dad shuffled through the doorway to the living room.

He scowled at her. "You should have woken me before the guests started arriving."

"Let it go, Ethan," Jo said. "You needed the sleep."

"And here's some coffee," Audrey Fryer pressed a steaming mug into Dad's hand.

"You're our guest. I don't expect you to serve me on your day off." However, Dad accepted the cup and took a sip before he looked around the kitchen. "Where's Donny?" He frowned. "For that matter, where's Kirsten?"

"Chief Hall called right before the Fryers arrived." Kaley hugged herself. She couldn't have faced this Stedman even if he was in handcuffs. Not with the sheer hatred in his expression and aura every time she'd seen him over the last three days. "The enforcers have come up with a plan for interrogating River's stalker, but Chief Hall couldn't talk about it over the phone."

"But she and Jimmy were going to do that last night," Dad protested.

Kaley shrugged. "I don't know what to tell you. Kirsten and Donny didn't know anything when they left."

"Pat's a smart cookie." Audrey smiled. "If she's got a plan, I trust her to make it work."

Dad scowled. "My wife's life and freedom are on the line, so excuse me for wanting something to happen now."

Mr. Harper grunted. "Ethan, I know you want Rachel home,

but there's more than a couple of law enforcement folks who agree with Humanity Now's ideas. Chief Hall will protect both the department's reputation and safeguard Rachel. That's going to take her some time." He turned to Kaley. "Unless you've got a spell that can speed up the process?"

"If I did, I would have already cast it—"

Loud pounding came from the living room. Kaley exchanged looks with Dad.

"The Fairbanks?" he asked.

"No." But she couldn't tell who was at the front door past the thick, choking fear.

More pounding. Dad strode out of the kitchen, and Kaley scurried after him. He yanked open the front door.

Mrs. Stillwell stood on the welcome mat, shivering in her insulated parka. David loomed over his mom.

"Where's my daughter?" Mrs. Stillwell demanded.

Chapter 22

Kirsten stood next to Police Chief Hall in the darkened recording room and watched Detective Mercer and Chief Enforcer Lambert through the one-way glass while they questioned Burt Stedman. They could hear everything in the interrogation room, but Stedman couldn't hear them. However, Chief Hall could talk to Mercer and Lambert through the earpieces the two law officers wore. At the desk on the other side of Chief Hall, Ellie was on her laptop, searching every reference Stedman gave. She looked supernatural herself at the speed she was typing.

Mom may still be sitting in a holding cell, but this was a step closer to finding Simon's killer and getting Mom released.

The background check the chief handed to Kirsten showed Stedman was from Akron. He'd been honorably discharged from the Army, but the record insinuated the discharge had been for medical reasons. However, there were no specific details due to privacy laws. Maybe it had something to do with his only sibling's death.

After Mercer read Stedman his rights on the record, the detective reiterated Stedman's right to an attorney.

Stedman shook his head. He seemed resigned to his fate.

"How long have you been a member of Humanity Now?" The mic distorted Mercer's voice. But part of the change was his deliberate deepening of his tone.

"A year." Stedman seemed self-assured for someone who had been picked up for stalking and a possible person of interest in a murder. "But I don't believe in their cause."

"Then why join them?"

Stedman rubbed the scars on his hand before he looked up at the detective. "They murdered my sister."

"Who?" Lambert asked.

"Humanity Now," Stedman replied. Well, that explained his weird behavior.

"Is your sister a supernatural?" Lambert asked.

Stedman shook his head.

"Mr. Stedman, I need you to answer verbally for the record," Mercer said.

"No," Stedman snapped. "Neither am I."

Mercer's bushy graying eyebrows drew together. "What purpose would it serve by Humanity Now killing a Normal?"

"I think they used Sheila to try to start a race war." Stedman shrugged. "She was pretty. Blond. A student at the University of Akron. They tried to make it look like a werewolf did it. I'd gotten leave and was going to surprise her. Instead, I interrupted the attacker, and he shoved me through the sliding glass door of her apartment."

He waved at his scars on his right hand. "Except I couldn't get anyone to believe me. This was a year after the Rainier Outing when people still thought the footage from the Seattle eruption and tsunami was faked."

"What did the Akron police say?" Mercer asked.

"They hit a dead end. Chalked it up to a crazy supernatural wannabe." Stedman's careful calm shattered. His body shook, and rage poured off him. Kirsten shivered from the intensity of his emotions. She didn't know how Lambert dealt with being that close to him.

Their suspect grimaced at his memories. "But I kept at it. She had died in my arms, and I didn't want her killer to get away."

"What makes you believe Humanity Now was involved?" Detective Mercer asked.

"There's places online." Stedman shifted in his chair, and his handcuffs rattled. "Places where people post some awful shit.

There was a snuff video. A man wore the same fake werewolf outfit in the recording as the guy who attacked my sister. Except when he was . . . done with his victim, he pulled the mask off, and it was Warren Simon."

Kirsten looked at Chief Hall.

She scowled. "Jill, have him give you the IP address so we can find this site."

Chief Enforcer Lambert repeated Chief Hall's request. As Stedman rattled off the address, Ellie's rapid-fire typing entered it into her computer.

"Be careful," Kirsten whispered. "We've got no idea what kind of viruses may be on that site."

Ellie grinned though she didn't take her eyes from her screen. "Both I and my baby use protection at all times."

Kirsten bit her cheek to stop any snarky remarks. Nothing that came to mind was suitable in front of her future employer.

"If you don't believe in Humanity Now's objectives, how'd you get them to accept you?" Mercer asked.

"I studied known members' social media, and then I created an account to look like someone they'd recruit." Stedman shrugged. "I waited nearly three years before an Army acquaintance contacted me. I thought he just wanted to reminisce about old times, but after a month, he asked me about my account. I told him my sister was killed by a were, and the police hadn't done jack shit."

"Who's this army buddy?" Mercer asked.

"His name's Trey Bower. There's a picture of him on my contacts page in my phone."

"Chief?" Ellie turned her laptop toward Hall. The Bower guy's photo was displayed on the screen. "Already sent a copy to you, the sheriff, and Chief Enforcers Lambert and Robbins. What's Mercer's number?"

Chief Hall's phone beeped in the middle of Ellie's recitation.

"I'll forward the photo to him and cc you." She pulled her phone off her equipment belt, and her fingers danced over the surface.

"Why didn't you call one of the supernatural legal resources in Cleveland?" Lambert asked.

"Why would your coven help me?" Stedman shrugged again. "You people know when someone's lying. Since I know my sister wasn't killed by a supernatural, you or the vamp would have told me it's not your problem."

Crap. He was right. That's exactly what the enforcers would have told him. A Normal crime was under Normal jurisdiction.

And Lambert knew it, too, from the blush creeping up her neck.

"Anyway, after a few weeks of hanging out, he introduced me to some folks at the Akron chapter." Stedman snorted, and his disgust tasted like rotten sour cream at the back of Kirsten's throat. "I made a point of bringing up the video, and asked them if the woman was a supernatural. They said she was someone who dated a supernatural. They needed to make examples of humans who mixed with the enemy."

Ellie muttered a swear word, but her anger was directed at Humanity Now's policies. And according to the organization, Kirsten, Kaley, Donny, and River shouldn't exist.

"Did your sister have a romantic relationship with a supernatural?" Lambert asked in a sympathetic voice.

"If the boy she was seeing was a supernatural, she either didn't know or she was afraid to tell me." Stedman's aura faded to a grayish-red, and he exhaled his grief. For an instant, Kirsten felt sorry for him. "His name is Lance Durham."

Chief Enforcer Lambert froze in her chair. Ellie typed in the name Stedman gave for his sister's boyfriend, but Kirsten didn't need the research. "He's now Brown Dog's Lesser Fire Elder."

The coven had given Mom so much crap about marrying Dad

years ago. It was a wonder the Elders hadn't made rules against dating Normals before Elder Durham's college girlfriend was killed.

Mercer must have realized Lambert knew something, but he couldn't ask in front of their suspect. He changed the subject. "Why were you following River Martin around town?"

"Vicki assigned me to watch him." Stedman grimaced. "The Indianapolis chapter targeted the kid and one of his teachers since they were both supernaturals. The kid managed to escape."

"Who's Vicki?" Mercer asked.

"Vicki Foster. Simon's second-in-command."

Kirsten leaned closer to the microphone. "The dark-haired lady with Simon on the street when he faced off with Jo and Mom on Monday."

Detective Mercer opened his folder and handed Stedman a photo from Monday's protest. "This lady?" He tapped a face on the picture.

"Yeah," Stedman answered.

"What was the teacher's name in Indianapolis?" Lambert asked.

"Wesley Crawford."

A chill ran down Kirsten's spine. Had River's mom gone to the Humanity Now people in Indianapolis for help in killing Mr. Crawford?

Chapter 23

"Hope's not here, Mrs. Stillwell," Kaley blurted. "What's going on?"

Mrs. Stillwell's voice shook. "W-we had a fight. She stormed out of the house last night."

"She didn't take her Jeep," David added. "Dad and I have been all over the farm, but we can't find her."

"Come in," Dad said. "We'll get you some coffee. Have you made a missing person report to the police or sheriff's departments?"

Mrs. Stillwell glanced Kaley and hesitated. David gently pushed his mom in the small of her back. "It's too damn cold to talk on their porch, Mom."

He looked up at Dad. "No, we haven't called them yet, and Hope isn't answering her own phone. As tight as Hope and Kirsten are, I assumed she had come here last night and turned off her phone. It's my fault. I told Mom and Dad to give her some space."

Mrs. Stillwell entered the house, followed by David. Dad closed the front door. The mix of the chill outside air and the kitchen's hot and humid atmosphere formed icy condensation on the intact living room windows.

Noticing all the faces poking out from the kitchen and dining room, Mrs. Stillwell blushed. "You're having Thanksgiving dinner with everything going on in town?"

"Yes, we are," Kaley said sternly. "Even with our troubles, we're thankful for our friends and family. When was the last time any of you saw Hope?"

"Around eight p.m." David pulled a clear plastic bag from his coat pocket. It contained a blue brush with long blond hairs. "I hate to ask a personal favor, Kaley, but could you or Kirsten cast a tracking spell?"

Kaley nodded and accepted the bag.

"Wait." Jo strode over to them. "Let me."

Kaley blinked in confusion. "Why?"

"After some of the crap happening in Millersburg, I don't want to risk your life," she said. "I'm too old and crotchety to kill."

"Wait a minute," Mrs. Stillwell demanded. "Where's Kirsten?"

"She's with my son Donny," Audrey Fryer said hotly. "They're running a last-minute errand. Not everyone wasted their week marching in front of the courthouse with a bunch of jerks who are trying to take away my son's future."

Audrey's vehemence drove Mrs. Stillwell back into her son's chest.

"Easy." Dad laid a palm on Audrey's shoulder. "Our concern here is Hope's well-being." He eyed Mrs. Stillwell. "And frankly, Lucy, if Hope had showed up here, I would have called you."

"Just like he did when River came here because some Humanity Now asshole was stalking us yesterday," Miz Cissy snapped.

Red bloomed upwards from Mrs. Stillwell's white scarf to the tips of her graying roots. "Maybe they wouldn't be suspicious of him if he didn't hang out with witches!"

"Mom, stop it!" Anger flooded from David.

"It's all right, man." River's smile was downright scary. "It's not my first rodeo with folks who believe I'm a second-class citizen." Shadows flowed where they couldn't be in the living room and the temperature dropped. Kaley shivered between the rasp of fae magick and the suddenly frigid air.

"River, what have I said about not blowing up my house?" Dad said wearily.

"Sorry, Doctor Wilson." Except River didn't sound one bit sorry though he did quell his powers. "Kaley, why don't you and your aunt go upstairs and cast that tracking spell? I don't want anything to happen to Hope."

Kaley headed for the stairs, Jo on her heels. She hoped Dad could keep things calm downstairs.

But the same uneasy feeling that had plagued her all week came back in a rush. She shot a quick prayer to the Goddess they found Hope before something really did happen to the Lady Knights center.

# Chapter 24

Kirsten relayed her concerns about Heather Martin obtaining the knowledge of mixed magick from Humanity Now to Chief Hall.

The police officer grimaced. "Or maybe River's mom cut a deal with Humanity Now to kill Crawford in return for allowing her to leave Indianapolis with her son."

"She's a Normal," Kirsten added. "She had to learn how to create her mixed-magick bombs from someone. Did Simon know about the bombs? Or did he teach Heather?"

Chief Enforcer Lambert's lips twitched when Chief Hall relayed their theories. Had the same ideas crossed the other witch's mind?

"Mr. Stedman, is this your wallet?" Detective Mercer held up an evidence bag.

Their suspect frowned and nodded. "It looks like mine. But your people took it when I was arrested. Why is it in a bag that says 'evidence'?"

"What about this one?" Mercer fished out a second evidence bag from the huge manila envelope in his lap. The clear plastic showed another wallet, a nearly exact duplicate of the first one. Both wallets showed similar light wear. Creases in the leather. Worn corners.

Stedman looked up at the detective. "What's going on here?"

"Which one is your wallet, Mr. Stedman?" Mercer laid the second bag next to the first one.

The suspect stared at the two bags for a long moment before he closed his eyes and swore a blue streak. "She set me up."

"Who set you up?" Lambert asked.

"Vicki Foster." Stedman sagged in his chair and opened his

eyes. "Let me guess. You found one of the wallets on Simon's body. Right?"

Neither law officer spoke.

Stedman straightened. "I'll accept whatever charges you file. You have my complete cooperation in taking down Foster and the rest of Humanity Now for what they did to my sister."

Chief Hall leaned toward the microphone. "Let's bring in Donny."

Kirsten felt a little bad about this plan. But on the other hand, he did look cute in his K-9 bulletproof vest and its matching collar and leash.

K-9 Officer Mary Beth Grassley of the Holmes County Sheriff's Department walked with Donny into the room. He wagged his tail as they circled the two officers and their suspect. Donny and the officer stopped to the right of Stedman.

"What the hell kind of dog is that?" Their suspect eyed Donny suspiciously.

"He's with the sheriff's department, and that's all you need to know," Mercer drawled in his best redneck accent. "Now, once again—" He held up both bags. "—do you know which wallet is yours?"

"I don't know—" He hesitated. "Vicki sat in the car while I ran into the pharmacy a couple of days ago. I was next at the check-out counter and dropped my wallet. Rachel Wilson picked it up and handed it back to me."

"Where you following Ms. Wilson like you were following River Martin?" Lambert asked.

"I wasn't." Stedman cocked his head. "It doesn't mean Vicki didn't have someone else tailing her. She must have seen me drop my wallet and—" His dark eyes widened. "You found my wallet with the witch's fingerprints on Simon's body, didn't you?"

"Either he's part of the plan and trying to lead us on, or he's not the brightest crayon in the box," Chief Hall murmured.

There was one way to find out. Kirsten leaned closer to the microphone. "Chief Enforcer, ask him what he was buying at Mast Pharmacy."

Lambert repeated the question.

Hot pink flashed through Stedman's maroon aura as the same time he blushed furiously. "I was buying condoms."

Lambert rolled her eyes, and both Chief Hall and Ellie chuckled.

"Are you sleeping with Foster?" Mercer asked.

"Yes," Stedman said sheepishly. "I thought I could use her for information. Apparently, she decided to use me to cover her tracks."

"Nice call, Kirsten," Ellie said.

Lambert faced Mercer. Despite his initial surprise, he adapted quickly to speaking telepathically. Conversation buzzed inside of Kirsten's brain as the chief enforcer asked the Normal detective to finish his initial questions. They needed to find Vicki Foster before she left Holmes County.

Detective Mercer turned back to their suspect and stared intently at him. "Mr. Stedman, did you kill Warren Simon?"

"No, I wanted to for what Humanity Now did to my sister, but someone beat me to it." A single tear trickled down Stedman's face.

"Do you know who did kill Warren Simon?"

"No." Stedman shook his head. "All I have are suspicions. No facts."

"Kid?"

The werecoyote barked twice. Stedman was telling the truth.

Kirsten's phone vibrated in her pocket. Kaley probably couldn't find the recipe for the turkey gravy. Why didn't she ask Jo? Surely their great-aunt was at their house by now. Kirsten yanked out her phone and checked the message. Yep, Kaley. But her sister's text triggered an ugly feeling in Kirsten's gut after Burt Stedman's testi-mony during his interrogation.

Hope was missing, and she was pretty and blond.

Just like Stedman's sister and the girl from the video he'd watched.

Chapter 25

Kaley pulled the wooden box Mom had gifted to her when she had turned thirteen from beneath her bed. The storage unit had a rich golden oak patina with brass hinges and lock. Her twin had been given a similar one, but Kirsten's was red-tinged mahogany.

Jo sat on the fake fur area rug and waited patiently. Or that's how it looked by her exterior. However, her mood was jumpier than Penn when he was high on catnip.

Kaley's bedroom door opened again, but instead of River, David stepped inside with a scowl on his face.

"I'm not trying to be nosy, but my mom's a lot safer with me up here."

From the screeching downstairs, Kaley didn't blame him.

"Just sit on the bed and keep your mouth shut while we do this. By the way, where's your father?" Jo said while Kaley removed a pewter bowl and a vial of sage oil from her storage box.

"He drove over to the Burkes." David's sigh was louder than the creak of Kaley's bedframe. "We were afraid if we called Kirsten or Olivia and Hope was with either friend, she might take off again."

"Ethan really would have called your parents if your sister showed up here," Jo said. "The Burkes would have as well."

"Either way, Hope's not the type to run away from a problem," Kaley murmured.

"I know." David crossed his arms. "That's why I'm worried."

When Kaley removed Hope's brush from the plastic bag, her aunt held out her hand.

Kaley shook her head. "Jo, I know you're concerned about my safety—"

"Plus, I've got more experience." Jo waggled her fingers.

"But I know her better," Kaley said. "According to one of my teachers, a personal connection to the missing person or object can sometimes overcome any block."

Jo's eyes narrowed at Kaley's gentle mockery. "You don't think Hope is hiding on purpose."

"Aren't you the one who says there's no such thing as a coincidence?" Kaley shot back.

"You think someone may have taken her?" David asked incredulously.

Kaley looked up at him. "She's worked at the coffee shop for the last couple of days, and she stands out in a crowd."

"Hope wouldn't have gone quietly if someone tried to kidnap her." David's aura flared a brilliant crimson.

"Normally, I'd agree with you." Kaley plucked a few hairs from the brush and dropped them in her metal bowl before she replaced it in the plastic bag. "But a couple of weeks ago, we had a Normal using magick bombs to blow up places."

David grimaced. "Yeah, Mom told me about the Painter Building and the attempt at the high school. It's part of her going off about—" He blushed. "She never had a problem with you guys before Humanity Now started their hate campaign."

"Yeah," Kaley said dryly. "Like assuming Kirsten would kill the entire girls basketball team for no reason. They are all bound and determined to go to the state tournaments this year. Playing basketball is one of the few things that makes my sister feel like a Normal." She uncorked her vial and poured a few drops of sage oil on the hairs in the bowl.

"Maybe I should—" Jo started.

"Are you doubting your teaching abilities?" Kaley eyed her.

"I'm doubting your desire to practice your gifts on a regular basis," Jo snapped.

Kaley stared at her aunt. There had been a time when she had blown off her craft lessons, but watching River stumble over his abilities because he had no one to show him how to safely control his fae magick made her realize what a fool she had been. And the last thing she wanted was to get into another fight with her aunt over River.

The silence dragged on until Jo sighed. She shook her head. "Fine."

That one word was the only admission and apology Kaley would receive, but damn, she'd take it. Because the weird nausea and anxiousness both she and Kirsten had experienced over the last four days was getting worse.

Kaley concentrated. Her right palm heated until a tiny flame flickered in her cupped hand. A tingling crawled up her spine from David watching her. She didn't remember such nervousness when she threw up a ward to protect Coach Cross and the other cheerleaders from Noah Eisler's dream form. Maybe the difference was the pure adrenaline at the blue dream coyote's attack.

She dropped the flame into the bowl. The oil caught fire, and Hope's hairs blackened and hissed as they burned. Kaley murmured the words of the spell.

A golden strand of energy swirled above the dying flames. It uncoiled, and one end wrapped itself around her right wrist. The other end shot through the north wall of her room.

"Did it work?" David murmured. Of course, he couldn't See the tracking spell.

"Yep." Kaley grinned at him.

"How far?" Jo asked.

Kaley felt for the other end of energy line. "Around five miles."

He jumped to his feet. "Grab your coat. I'll drive."

"No." Jo stood. "I'll take her."

"Normal problems call for Normal solutions." He reached under the back of his coat and produced a handgun. "Besides, it's probably an ambush for you gals. I'd leave Kaley here if I could." He replaced his weapon and charged for the bedroom door.

"I hate to say it, but he's right," Kaley admitted. She pushed to her feet and followed David out of her room. But it wouldn't hurt to have some backup, and she knew just who to call.

Chapter 26

Kirsten relayed her twin's text to Chief Hall. Before the chief could answer, Ellie's phone chimed. The St. James enforcer checked her message.

"Kaley's tracking Hope, and she wants me to back them up," Ellie said. "They believe Hope may have been kidnapped by members of Humanity Now."

Chief Hall frowned. "If they have, they'll be expecting the local supernaturals to rescue her. Let my people handle this."

"And what if Officer Zarnecki or someone else in the police or sheriff's departments are feeding Humanity Now information?" Ellie countered.

Chief Hall's eyes narrowed at the implied insult, even though she had the same concerns. "Why does Kaley want you in particular?"

"Because Ellie's a Normal enforcer, which is probably the reason David's with Kaley and not Aunt Jo," Kirsten answered. "Do you need me and Donny for anything else?"

"One moment." The chief held up her right index finger before she leaned closer to the mic. "Ask Stedman if Simon had picked out a female victim to pull the same stunt with as he did with Stedman's sister."

Chief Enforcer Lambert leaned her elbows on the table. "Did Simon tag a local Normal girl to kill like he did your sister?"

Stedham nodded. "But all Vicki knew was that he planned to kill one of the Normal high school basketball players and blame it on the werecoyote who attends the school." At Donny's low growl, Stedman shot him a suspicious look.

Chief Hall snorted. "Well, that gives us enough to bring Vicki

Foster in for questioning, but we're no closer to finding Simon's killer."

"Let us find Hope. You'll have cause to bust the people responsible, and you can question them," Kirsten said. "But right now, the proverbial clock's ticking."

"Keep me apprised of your status." Chief Hall turned to Ellie. "Both of you."

"Do you mind if we keep Donny in his K-9 vest?"

Chief Hall grinned. "Of course not. Sheriff Birkheimer ordered it especially for him."

Kirsten frowned. "He plans on treating him like a regular canine officer."

Chief Hall chuckled. "Deputy Wolford suggested it since Donny's constant shifting was uncomfortable for him, and we wouldn't have to worry about finding him a safe spot to change."

For a split second, Kirsten's confidence faltered. "Are you offering him the internship instead of me?"

"No, an offer has been made to both of you." Chief Hall smiled in genuine reassurance. "During the investigation into the Painter Building bombing, you two made a good team."

Behind the chief, Ellie made a gagging gesture with her right index finger.

Kirsten didn't give the enforcer the satisfaction of a reaction. Chief Hall's statement didn't make sense. The mayor and county commissioners had only assigned funds for one supernatural officer and one supernatural intern. Had recent events made the local officials change their minds about their recruiting plan? And why hadn't Donny said anything to her about being offered the second internship? When the Chief and Uncle Jimmy made the offer to her back in October, they said they only had one intern position for the taskforce, and one of the requirements was taking college classes. How could Donny pay for those classes if he lost his football scholarship?

"We'll discuss the internships after you find Hope," Chief Hall prodded.

Guilt poured through Kirsten. Damn, she was being selfish. Hope was her best friend. And Kirsten prayed her fellow Lady Knight was okay. But that week-long nagging itch along Kirsten's nerves was getting worse. She grabbed her coat and slung it on. Ellie already had her equipment packed and was donning her own coat.

"I'll text you once we know something," Kirsten said.

Chief Hall merely nodded and resumed watching Stedman's interrogation. Kirsten charged out of the observation room.

She raised her fist to knock on the interrogation room door when Ellie grabbed Kirsten's arm and yanked her to a halt. "Hey."

"What?" Kirsten ground out as she whirled to yell at the enforcer.

Ellie dragged her away from the door and halfway down the hall. "Can you keep your emotional issues with Donny on hold until we find Hope?" Ellie's piercing blue eyes bore into Kirsten.

"My emotional issues?" She deliberately crowded into Ellie's personal space, but the enforcer didn't back away.

"I may not have your telepathic abilities, but your body language says you have some weird love/hate thing going on with that particular were." Ellie shrugged. "Normally, I'd wave that crap off as none of my business, but we're going into a possible retrieval mission, and I need your head clear."

Kirsten blinked. Ellie was right. About everything.

She sucked in a deep breath. "You're right. I can keep it together."

"What's your element, and what's Kaley's?"

"I'm a water witch," Kirsten said. "My sister's an air witch."

A wicked smile lit up the enforcer's face. "You good with altering the temperature of water?"

"Yes." Kirsten wasn't rude enough to delve into Ellie's mind. "You have an idea?"

"Yeah."

Behind them, the interrogation room door opened. They both turned to find Officer Grassley exiting the room with Donny.

"Sorry about the leash, dude." Grassley released Donny with a snap of the clip. "I kinda wish my Libbie was a were. It would be so much easier if she understood more than a few words of English."

Donny's tongue lolled out of his mouth in a canine grin before he trotted down to Kirsten and nudged her hand with his furry head. *Let's get the jerks who kidnapped Hope.*

"We only know she's missing," Kirsten murmured.

Your aunt Jo always says there's no such thing as a coincidence, he replied.

His words sent another pulse through her overwrought nerves. She sent another quick prayer to the Goddess they found Hope before anything happened to her.

Chapter 27

Kaley concentrated on her tracking spell, calling out turns on the truck's GPS app, while David drove like a maniac over the winding county and township roads.

Kaley? We need your location.

Her twin's mental voice sent a twinge of reassurance through Kaley. She relayed their current route and direction.

We're on our way—holy crap!

Kaley wanted to scream, but she didn't dare blow her sister's concentration.

Sorry about that, Kirsten said. *Some jerk must be hunting early because an entire herd of deer just darted in front of us. You okay, Donny?*

Someone needs to develop a seatbelt I can unlatch with a paw, the 'coyote growled as he climbed back up on the rear passenger seat of Ellie's SUV.

Kaley couldn't help the giggle that burbled out of her.

David shot her an annoyed glance. "This situation isn't funny."

"No, it isn't," she replied calmly. "But we have backup on the way."

"Jimmy and some of the deputies?"

"Better." Kaley grinned. "A trained enforcer from a vampire coven, a werecoyote, and my sister who's pissed someone may have kidnapped her best friend." She sobered. "Slow down. We're getting close."

David tapped his brakes. Thank Goddess, very few people were out and about on the roads because of the holiday. They'd only passed three vehicles in their mad dash out of town.

Kaley concentrated on the golden thread of magick connecting her and Hope. "She's at the old Clay place."

"I'll park at the entrance to the archery range." David glanced at her again. "Unless you can hex the padlock? That way I can stop out of sight of the road."

Kaley nodded. "Not a problem." Last month, she'd been a little envious of Uncle Jimmy tapping her twin for the law enforcement internship. Now, she didn't think she would be able to handle such a position from the way her heart pounded.

David turned left into the dirt drive to the range. As soon as he braked, she jumped out of his pickup and raced over to the locked bars blocking anyone from doing what they were about to do. A quick, muttered spell and the padlock popped open. She jerked it out of the way and pushed the right bar back so there was room for a vehicle to pass.

David eased his pickup through the opening. Kaley pushed the bar back in place and secured the padlock only to the right bar. Anyone glancing at the gate from the township road would assume the entrance was still secure. She ran back to the pickup and climbed into the passenger seat.

He nodded at her. "Have you thought about joining the Marines? We could use someone like you."

She laughed. "Thanks for the vote of confidence, but I'm not shaving my head for anyone. Not even Uncle Sam."

He chuckled as he drove a half mile up the trail and pulled off to the side. His pickup would be invisible unless someone came traipsing through the woods. She relayed their location and the terminus of the tracking spell to Kirsten before she opened the truck door once again and jumped down from passenger seat.

"You stay here while I scout the situation," David said.

"No." Kaley cocked her head, listening to Ellie's plan. "We wait for the other three. Kirsten and I will provide cover for all of us."

Before she could say more, they heard an engine behind them. David drew his gun, but it was the St. James party's silver SUV. Kaley placed a hand on David's arm, and he lowered his weapon.

Ellie parked behind David's pickup. Kaley released David as Kirsten's group climbed out of the SUV.

Donny trotted up to Kaley. *What do you think of my new duds?* He pranced like he was runway model to show all the angles.

"Did you raid Libbie's equipment locker?" Kaley teased.

Nope, these are mine. I'm an official member of the K-9 Corps.

He was way too proud of himself. She looked at Kirsten who wore a sour expression. Oh, crap. What did Donny's new position mean for her sister's internship?

Kirsten gave a slight shake of her head. *We'll discuss this later.*

Kaley turned to David. "Is it okay if I link you to the rest of us?" She waved at the other three teens. "That way we can communicate without making noise."

"Telepathy?" He frowned.

She nodded.

"I'm not sure I want to expose you to some of the things . . ." A worried expression fell over his features.

"It's a surface link, man," Ellie said. "We just hear each other in our heads." She tapped her temple. "And I'm not trying to one-up you, but I've had my own share of terrible, bloody situations. If I can keep control in a link, you can, too."

Relief spread over David's face. "What do I need to do?"

Kaley touched his arm again. *Nothing.*

Whoa! David blinked, but it was from surprise and a touch of pleasure. *You sure I can't talk you into a civilian contract with my unit?*

Dude, I'm just a high school cheerleader, Kaley replied. *Besides, there are rules about supernaturals fighting Normal battles.*

"And right now, we need to find Hope," Kirsten added sharply.

"Ellie, you know basic CQB?" David asked.

The enforcer nodded. No sarcastic quips from her this time. Good to know she was taking this whole thing seriously.

Kaley led the way through the woods, following her tracking spell. Donny trotted beside her, sniffing the detritus they trod on for any clue. At least, the older woods had soaked up the rain from Tuesday so they weren't wading through mud like she, Kirsten, and Donny had been at the Christmas tree farm yesterday afternoon.

There's been people through here in the last couple of days, he remarked.

Is the archery range open this late in the year? Ellie asked.

Only by appointment, Kirsten replied.

Or whoever is at the old Clay place has been doing recon around the property, David said.

The woods grew a little brighter. Kaley dropped to a crouch and eased up to dead milkweed stalks marking the transition from the woods to the farmhouse yard. The other three bipeds followed her motions. Donny belly-crawled next to her. Yep, the tracking spell definitely stopped at the old farmhouse in front of them.

What had been white paint on the exterior had turned grayish under the constantly changing Ohio weather. Darker gray stained the wood plank siding where the pain had peeled off. The roof of the front porch dipped precariously where the pillar on the south side had rotted away. Overgrowth clogged the land around the house. The gravel drive still existed, though the weeds were doing their best to reclaim the territory.

However, the barn was in much better shape. Its maroon paint wasn't fresh, but it had been applied within a decade. The latch and locks didn't show the same rust the gutters of the house did. And the patch of weeds in front of the two huge rolling doors had been mowed sometime in late summer.

At least, we don't have to worry about snakes this time of the year while we wade through the yard, Kirsten mused.

Ellie glanced up at the low, overcast sky. *Is there enough moisture in the air for you to work with?*

No problem. Kirsten looked at Kaley. *Ready?*

She nodded and concentrated. She warmed the air around them while her twin tugged on the water droplets in the clouds above them. Fog swirled and thickened as it blanketed the farm house and barn. By the time she and Kirsten were done, Kaley could barely see Donny next to her.

Kirsten squeezed Kaley's shoulder. *Hold it as long as you can.*

Find Hope. Kaley showed her sister the terminus on the second floor of the farmhouse before she sat down on the damp weeds. All she needed to do was hold the dome of fog over the Clay property until the rest of the team could get Hope out of the farmhouse and back to the edge of the woods.

Easy, right?

Chapter 28

Damp air filled Kirsten's lungs as she raced after Donny and David through the weeds surrounding the old Clay farmhouse. The fog she and Kaley had summoned muffled their steps. To her surprise, Ellie kept up with her. Maybe the enforcer didn't totally rely on her family's money and her position within the coven after all.

By unspoken consensus, no one trusted the partially collapsed front porch. They headed for the back door. Both David and Ellie drew their weapons and stood on each side of the door frame.

Kirsten? Ellie asked as she tried the back door. It was locked.

Two Normals on the second floor. I don't detect anyone else, she replied.

Ellie waited until Donny was beside David before she nodded.

The marine kicked the door. The dry-rotted doorjamb crumbled from the force, and the door itself slammed open. Kirsten threw up a ward in front of him, but no one was in the kitchen.

The instant she dropped her shield, Donny ran inside and sniffed the peeling linoleum. *It's Hope's scent all right. And one other person's is the most recent. Normal female. Can't identify who it is though.*

We still clear the ground floor. Ellie looked over her shoulder at Kirsten. *Don't throw any fireballs. This place would go up like flashpaper.*

I wouldn't if I could, she snapped back.

Still, she stayed close behind Ellie as she and David quickly swept the downstairs rooms. Whoever was inside the house would know they were here from the noise of David kicking in the back door. But if Humanity Now was somehow dealing in magick . . .

Kirsten shoved the disturbing thought aside. She needed to focus on the here and now.

David took the lead and climbed the stairs to the second story two at a time. The wood groaned and squeaked from his heavy tread. Not that the lighter footsteps of the rest of the group put any less stress on the century-old planks.

Last bedroom, Kirsten and Donny said at the same time.

No magick other than the tracking spell, she added.

However, David and Ellie cleared the other three bedrooms before they advanced to the last one at the front of the house. Donny slipped in front of the bipeds and entered the room with a low growl.

"Don't come closer!"

Kirsten recognized the voice, but she peeked around the doorjamb to confirm her suspicions.

In the middle of the room, Vicki Foster stood next to a seated Hope, who looked ready to tear the Humanity Now member into bits if she were loose. Kirsten's best friend looked like a silver mummy with all the duct tape wrapped around her entire body and the chair she was secured to. But it was the gold Celtic knot on an earring fishhook with quartz beads Vicki held that chilled Kirsten to her core. The blankness of the gold and stones told her exactly what was in the woman's hand.

"Stop," she hissed. "She's holding a mixed magick bomb."

Ellie muttered an obscenity under her breath. Donny growled again.

"I know what you are, you mangy bastard." Vicki sneered. "Even your vaunted healing ability won't survive this." She shook the charm.

The vague blankness of whatever kept the fae and witch magicks from interacting was the only reason Kirsten knew what Foster held. This one wasn't leaking like the ones River's mother had used around town. But Kirsten had no doubt the bomb Vicki held was just as dangerous if not more so.

Kirsten, can you defuse the bomb if I take her out? David asked.

Ellie responded first. *Those things can't be defused. The only way to get rid of it is to clear everyone and have a witch or fae trigger it from a safe distance. The only good thing is the baffle spell prevents temporary blindness and migraines in the magickal folks who might be nearby.*

Kirsten gritted her teeth. Ellie knew more about these damn bombs than she did. She'd have to pick the enforcer's brain if they survived this encounter.

She slipped past David and Ellie. They hissed at her both mentally and audibly to get back behind them, but Kirsten ignored them. The wood groaned ominously beneath her tennies. She stopped beside Donny and laid a hand on his furry head.

"Why do you want to die so badly, Vicki?" Kirsten murmured.

"If this kills you abhorrent brats, my death will be worth it," Vicki spat.

"Is that why you killed Warren?"

Grief mixed with Vicki's hate. "I didn't kill him. Burt Stedman did. The Wilson witch touched his wallet. H-he said it was a perfect opportunity to frame her. He planted it on Warren's body when he dumped it at the Christmas tree farm outside of Millersburg."

"How could Burt have killed Warren?" Kirsten cocked her head. "He died from a spell."

"I know." Tears trickled down Vicki's face. "He dropped a fae charm that speeds human metabolism into Warren's coffee. Warren has, had an irregular heartbeat so he only drank decaf. Between the fully caffeinated coffee and the charm, I think it triggered a heart attack."

Kirsten almost felt sorry for the woman, but she wasn't sure she totally believed Vicki Foster. Who did what and when was something for the county prosecutor to sort out. Kirsten's first priority needed to be her best friend.

She reached out and pulled Hope into their link. *You okay?*

Yeah, just get me out of this tape, and let me punch the bitch.

Kirsten sighed in relief. Hope was fine if she were this mad.

"Vicki, you can probably cut a deal if you release Hope now," Kirsten said. "This whole mess—"

"No!" A wild look flamed in Vicki's eyes. "I won't—"

"We know what Simon intended to do to Hope," David said brusquely. "Do you really think I'll let you—"

The floor beneath Kirsten's shoes trembled. The wood whined.

Donny! Get her out! Hope's silent warning came as the planks in the middle of the room cracked and splintered.

Donny jumped and knocked Kirsten over. He seized her left arm between his jaws and dragged her to the door. Desperately, she threw a ward around Hope.

All she could do was watch in horror as the floor opened up and swallowed her best friend and the very crazy Vicki Foster.

Chapter 29

Kaley felt rather than heard her twin's panic. She released the fog, jumped to her feet, and ran for the old Clay farmhouse.

At the roar that came from the house, she threw up a shield of condensed air. Through the lifting fog, window panes shattered on the front half of the building, and a cloud of dust rose from the multitude of empty holes. The south-eastern corner of the house sagged, and the front porch finished its collapse to the weed-infested yard.

Kirsten!

No answer. From anyone.

Kaley stopped, yanked her phone from her pocket, and punched in 9-1-1. She interrupted Betty Wolford's answering chirp. "This is Kaley Wilson. Get a rescue team and an ambulance out to the old Clay house on Township Road 59. There were six people on the second floor when part of it collapsed. Tell Chief Hall we found Hope Stillwell with Vicki Foster of Humanity Now."

"Stay on the line, Kaley," Betty said firmly.

"I will." Kaley held her coat sleeve over her nose and mouth as the dust cloud roiled over her. Goddess only knew how much asbestos might be in the ancient house. And if it was bad outside—

She concentrated, using air to carefully carry the dust clear of the house. As the particles settled in the weeds on the front lawn of the farmhouse, two grayish-white figures emerged from the back door, hacking up a storm. Only the size difference allowed her to recognize David and Ellie.

"Where's everybody else?" Kaley demanded.

Ellie bent over, sounding like she was about to disgorge her own lungs, but she pointed back at the house.

David spat black mucus onto the weeds. "Tried to get them out but they're digging Hope out of the debris. Call emergency—" He was interrupted by a massive coughing fit.

"I did." She handed her phone to Ellie who had collapsed on the ground. "They're on their way. Talk to Betty."

Kaley ran for the back door and entered the building. Despite her efforts, a thick layer of heavy particles covered every surface in the kitchen.

"Kirsten? Donny?"

A loud sneeze came from further in the house. It was followed by the clatter of wood on wood.

We're in the right front room, Kirsten answered. *Hope's under a ton of debris, and I need help.*

Kaley followed the noise. A woman sat in the hallway with Donny standing guard. Every time, she moved, even to cough, he growled deep in his chest.

Humanity Now? Kaley asked.

Yeah. He was furious, but she couldn't tell what specifically had raised his hackles other than the woman putting Kirsten and Hope in danger.

Kaley ducked beneath the cracked lintel into what had probably been the front parlor back when the house had been first built. Kirsten had wrapped her scarf around her nose and mouth. She worked feverishly, tossing aside broken planks and chunks of plaster. By her feet, Hope lay. She was covered in a thick layer of plaster dust and—duct tape?

"Help me," Kirsten commanded. "She fell when the upstairs floor collapsed. I threw up a ward around her, but all it did was cushion her landing a bit."

Between the dust and the duct tape, Hope was struggling to breathe.

Kaley peeled the tape from the girl's mouth. Despite being careful, Hope whimpered. Red marks and torn skin covered Hope's lower face.

"Better?" Kaley asked.

"Ch-chest and arms," Hope choked out before she started coughing from the dust Kirsten was stirring up trying to free her fellow Lady Knight.

Kirsten cleared enough debris from Hope that Kaley could see that the hands of the team's center had been taped behind the back slats of the chair before Hope had been taped to the chair itself. To top it off, Hope had landed on her back and arms.

Kaley didn't have a knife or scissors, so she whipped out her keychain. Her steel triquetra would do in a pinch. She stuck her hand underneath the hem of Hope's sweatshirt and held it up to protect the girl's skin and punctured holes in the tough tape. The holes in Hope's clothes didn't matter. The paramedics or ER personnel would end up cutting off her clothes in order to treat her. Goddess only knew how many of Hope's bones had broken when she landed despite Kirsten's ward. Kaley ripped apart the tape.

"Did one of you call emergency services?" Kirsten demanded as she cleared wood and plaster from Hope's legs.

"They're on their way," Kaley answered.

"Sorry for ruining your Thanksgiving," Hope murmured between coughs.

"These jerks framing Mom ruined our holiday," Kirsten bit out. "Not you."

We need to flip Hope on her side, Kaley said silently. The plaster dust was scraping her throat raw.

Kirsten hesitated. *I don't think we should move her.*

All of her weight is on her arms, Kaley protested. *It's cutting off her circulation.*

If you guys are trying to hide things from me, you might want to cut your telepathic link. Hope's giggle turned into another round of coughing.

Nope, Kaley said. *Just trying not to hack up a lung.*

"We have enough room," Kirsten said. "Let's set the chair upright."

Kaley shoved her keychain back into her front jeans pocket and grabbed the chair frame. The broken slats of the back were only held together by the mass of duct tape. "Ready."

Together, she and her twin heaved Hope and her chair onto the chair's feet. Hope hissed in pain.

First responders are on the way, Donny reported. *I can hear the sirens.*

"Now, get this duct tape off me," Hope said between gasps. "I need to beat the crap out of some Humanity Now jerks."

And have some mouthwash standing by because I need bite them, Donny said.

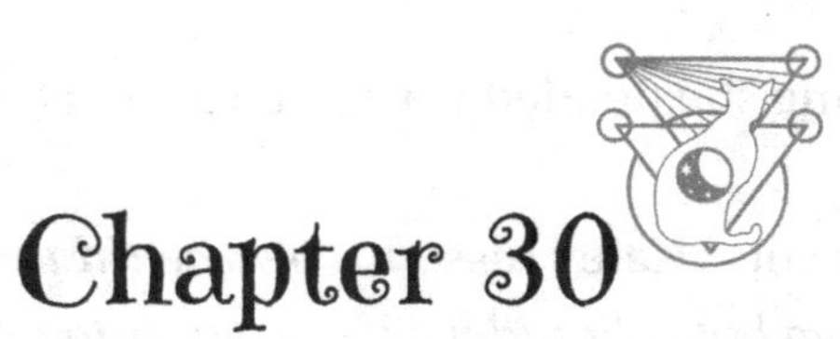

Chapter 30

In the end, neither Hope or Donny got their wishes.

As soon as law enforcement arrived at the Clay house, Vicki Foster tried to claim assault by the supernaturals and the crazy marine. She didn't get far. Hope called bullshit on her story loudly. When Foster argued that Hope was part of the conspiracy, Ellie pulled her phone out of her pocket and played Foster's confession, which she had the presence of mind to record while Kirsten had tried to talk Foster into releasing Hope.

Kirsten wanted to hug the West Coast enforcer.

When the ambulances arrived, Uncle Jimmy insisted anyone in the house when the floor collapsed needed to go to the hospital. When Donny complained through Kirsten, Uncle Jimmy threatened to take the 'coyote to the emergency vet clinic in Coshocton.

Donny dropped his protest.

Kirsten listened to her twin's spiel while she sat next to Kirsten's bed in the ER. Damn, they'd been to Pomerene Hospital way too often over the last couple of months.

"I called Dad and told him to bring River to the hospital," Kaley said. "Miz Audrey's on her way here, too."

"No, I don't want him healing me." Kirsten snapped. Her eyes still burned and itched from the powdered plaster even though one of the ER docs had washed out the grit. They'd also given her antibiotics for the minute scratches on her corneas and inner eyelids. Last thing she needed was to react to River's fae abilities in her irritation.

"Not for you," Kaley hissed. *I overheard the nurses saying Hope has dislocated both shoulders. If she wants to play the rest of this season, she needs him.*

Speak of the devil. Hope grinned at Kirsten as the orderly wheeled the star center past Kirsten's ER bay.

"Do me a favor, and grab a pop for me," Kirsten asked. "My throat's still sore as heck, and my mouth tastes like limestone and dead spiders."

"Since when do you eat spiders?" Kaley teased, but she stood and brushed past the curtain.

Kirsten heard her sister ask someone else if they wanted a pop. Donny requested a root beer.

Donny.

Kirsten rubbed her left bicep. The bruises from his teeth were already forming, but he hadn't broken the skin. If it weren't for his fast actions, she would have fallen through the collapsing floor, too.

Kaley was right. Kirsten gave Donny too much crap, yet she always went to him for help when her twin wasn't available. With a start, she realized jealousy wasn't the reason she didn't want him on the taskforce. She didn't want him to get hurt.

But what the hell was he going to do with his life if he lost his scholarship?

She threw off the nubby hospital blanket and slid out of her bed. With a firm grip on the back of the hospital gown she wore, she padded on bare feet to the bay next to hers.

"Knock, knock."

"Come on in," he called.

She slipped past the closed curtain and into the bay. Donny lay on a gurney exactly like hers, and he wore a matching hospital gown.

He blinked when he saw her. "Damn, your eyes look painful. I heard you had plaster bits in them."

"Yeah, but the tetanus shot I'm waiting for will be even more fun," she said. "That's what I get for digging through century-old plaster, wood, and nails. How're you doing?"

"Better than you girls," he said. "They just took Hope down to radiology."

"Kaley already called River." Kirsten shrugged. "I don't think Hope will miss any games."

Donny snorted. "What would we do without Honey Boy?"

"I'm more worried about what I'd do without you." Kirsten perched on the edge of the chair next to his bed. "Thanks for saving my ass back at the house."

He shrugged and looked everywhere but at her. "It was nothing."

"And I owe you a very big apology," she murmured.

His piercing brown eyes shot to her. "An apology for what? Being the closest person to the door?"

"No, for treating you like crap." She swallowed hard. "I didn't want to admit, not even to myself, I care about you."

His breath hitched. "What do you mean by caring about me?"

Goddess, this was so embarrassing. Maybe she'd been totally wrong about the clues he'd been giving.

"I was afraid if I said I-I . . . liked you, I'd be stuck in Millersburg forever."

"You're only stuck here if you want to be," he said softly. "But I would have followed you anywhere if we, uh, were . . . you know . . ."

"I couldn't ask that of you," she protested.

"What do I really have here?" he said bitterly. "I'm an outcast to the Killbuck pack. Not that I'd want to belong to that group of losers." He turned away for a moment. "The Las Vegas pack mistress tendered an offer to me to join them."

"Julia's stepmom?"

He nodded.

"Are you planning to accept it?" Damn, she didn't want to hear the answer now that she was being truthful with herself.

"I don't know." He inhaled sharply. "Do I have a reason to stay here next year besides Mom?"

So, he wasn't going to admit the taskforce had offered an internship to him. However, his hopeful look said he'd do whatever she asked.

She sagged in the chair. "I don't want to hold you back. I know what it's like to get crap from my own kind over my parenthood. If there's a chance of you being accepted by another pack, to live with other werecoyotes—"

Donny scowled. "You know for a smart chick, you can be incredibly dense at times."

"What's that supposed to mean?" she shot back.

"I love you," he growled. "I've always loved you. If you don't feel the same, have the guts to admit it."

"I-I . . ." Kirsten ran her tongue over her lips. "I love you, too." She jumped to her feet and dashed out of his bay and back into hers. Her heart pounded wildly.

What had she said to him? What the heck had she just done?

Her phone beeped. But the text message was from Donny.

> Did you know you smell like roses whenever I'm around?

She texted back.

> What do you mean?

> That's what people smell like when they're in love.

Kristen chuckled. She may have been lying to herself for the last few years, but he'd always known how she really felt.

Chapter 31

Despite Dad's protests, Uncle Jimmy insisted Kirsten, Donny, and Ellie go back to the sheriff's office after they were released by the hospital and file their reports regarding Vicki Foster's arrest for kidnapping Hope since the three of them were relatively healthy. Before they left the hospital, Kirsten elicited a promise from Kaley that she and River would make sure Hope would be okay.

"Mother Coyote, if I'd known helping law enforcement involved homework, I never would have volunteered," Donny grumbled from the back seat of Ellie's SUV.

"I have to write end of shift reports," Ellie snapped. "So, quit being a whiny were. It's best to write things down, or type them up, while they're still fresh in your mind."

"Did you even get your high school diploma?" he asked abruptly.

Now, where did that question come from?

"No." Ellie sucked in a deep breath, but she hesitated in whatever she wanted to say and released the air. Was she embarrassed? After seeing the scars on her shoulder, Kirsten couldn't blame Ellie for not wanting to be around the airheads that comprised most teens these days.

"There's no shame in not graduating from high school," Kirsten said fiercely. "School's not for everyone, and there are other ways to get an education."

"What would you guys say if I finished school here?" Ellie said in a rush.

"Why would you want to?" Donny blurted.

"Because no one here knows who I am," Ellie said softly.

"Would your parents agree to that?" Kirsten asked. "Millersburg is in Dare territory."

"My stepdad Jake is on board." The dashboard lights illuminated Ellie's grimace in the dark. "He said he'd work on Mom."

"Well, I'm with Donny," Kirsten said. "Why here? You could go anywhere in St. James territory if you need to get out of L.A. for a while."

"Okay, if you want to know the truth, you're the first supers who haven't gotten freaked out about my heritage or tried to use me to get to my aunt and uncle," Ellie said. "And you're the closest I've had to real friends in a long time."

Empathy for the California enforcer filled Kirsten. "We like you, too, but where are you going to live? The Levys are cool, but you don't strike me as the type to live without wi-fi."

"I can rent an apartment or a house—"

"I can tell you right now, that won't sit well with the Wilsons, my mom, or River's grandma," Donny said dryly from the back seat. "Much less Miz Anne or any of her clan."

"But Anne, Colin, and the rest of the Levys know you folks and they know this area," Ellie said. "What could they possible object to?"

"Once Mom's out of jail, we can set up a video chat between your parents and mine and discuss—" Kirsten winced. "Crap, we didn't grab Mom's Thanksgiving dinner."

"Your dad will bring her dinner out to her once you and Kaley are both home." Donny reached up and patted Kirsten's shoulder.

She chewed on her lip. It wasn't fair Mom was still behind bars, even though the sheriff's department had both Vicki Foster and Burt Stedman in custody and their recorded confessions of their parts in Warren Simon's murder.

Maybe Kirsten should "encourage" the county prosecutor to

drop Mom's charges, so she could come home for the rest of the holiday weekend.

Don't even think about that again, Donny snapped.

Why? she bit back.

That's the fastest way to lose your internship and any scholarships you might get. And I never thought you were stupid enough to ruin the chances of improving Normal and supernatural relations in town.

Was she that easy to read? *I really hate it when you're right.*

Donny snickered.

Ellie didn't bother to ask what was going on.

And Kirsten swallowed her embarrassment at even thinking about violating someone's free will.

Kirsten finished her report first, so she grabbed some chips and a soda from the vending machine and wandered over to Julia Wolford's office. The deputy regaled her with the story of how Vicki Foster's booking had turned into massive entertainment.

Foster had freaked out when she met both Brown Dog's and Dare's chief enforcers and learned they were involved in the investigation of Warren Simon's murder. When she acted like she had insects crawling all over her from being so close to a vampire and a witch, Jimmy ordered her to be de-loused. Julia had fun hosing Foster down with the insecticide soap spray.

Kirsten laughed so hard at Julia's animated caricature of Foster that orange pop spurted from her nose.

At a knock on Julia's open door, Kirsten turned to find Chief Enforcer Robbins with Jimmy. She stood. "I'm sure you guys need to talk business."

"Stay." Chief Enforcer Robbins stepped into the room and

placed a hand on Kirsten's shoulder. The coolness of his flesh seeped through the clean sweatshirt Dad had brought to the hospital. "You did a very good job today, Ms. Wilson, and unlike your mother, you kept your head in a difficult confrontation."

He turned to the sheriff. "Jimmy, would you mind if I added one of my people to your taskforce?"

"Need to keep an eye on us?" Jimmy grinned.

"Actually, I think we could learn a thing or two from you," Robbins said. "Don't worry. It won't be a vampire. I plan on sending a Normal enforcer trainee from our coven, and we'll cover his costs."

"Family?" Kirsten asked.

Robbins nodded.

"I'll have to run it past Pat Hall," Jimmy mused. "But I don't think she'll have a problem."

"Has the ME had a chance to perform the autopsy on Simon?" Julia asked.

Jimmy nodded. "Yes, and they did find the tiny charm in his stomach. Lambert and Tyler found a bunch more in Foster's hotel room."

"They need to be careful—" Kirsten blurted.

"We're not fools, child," Robbins said gently. "We have our own halfling enforcer on payroll. She and Chief Enforcer Lambert have already split those charms that haven't been bonded. Chief Enforcer Stanton of St. James Coven has disposed of the mixed magick bombs, including the one in the debris of the house where Miss Stillwell was kept."

"And the supernatural enforcers involved will be called as expert witnesses if these cases go to trial," Jimmy said.

Kirsten frowned. "You sound like you don't think the prosecutor's office will bring charges."

"Oh, they'll bring them, but both Stedman and Foster will probably aim for a plea deal." Jimmy snorted, his disgust evident. "Humanity Now's attorney is still in town, but he refuses to act as their personal counsel. They'll have to wait until Monday before they can get public defenders."

"Tuesday," Julia corrected.

"Why Tuesday?" Robbins asked.

Jimmy and Julia were too busy laughing hysterically to answer him. He was too polite to read their minds.

"Ohio white-tail season starts on Monday," Kirsten said.

Robbins sighed and shook his head before he held his palm out to Kirsten. "Good work this week, Ms. Wilson." She returned his firm handshake.

He turned to Jimmy and shook the sheriff's hand as well. "Don't break up the band, Sheriff Birkheimer. These kids do good work."

"I won't." Jimmy grinned at him.

Once the vampire departed, Jimmy eyed Kirsten. "I've got one more job for you tonight."

Kirsten groaned. "With all due respect, I've had a tiny bag of chips since breakfast. Can I go home and grab some food first."

"This one will be quick, then you and Donny can head home." He waved for her to follow.

Kirsten resisted the urge to roll her eyes. She waved to Julia before she jogged after her godfather. He led her to the waiting area by the duty officer's desk.

Donny was pacing, but he stopped the minute they entered the area. "It's about time. I'm starving, and there'd better be some turkey leftover at your house."

"Wait a minute." Jimmy held up his index finger.

When one of the female deputies escorted Mom out of the jail, all the anxiety and fear rushed out of Kirsten in a flood of tears. She ran over and wrapped her arms around Mom.

Kirsten sniffed back the snot, loosened her hold, and turned back to Jimmy. "H-How—"

"After Stedman and Foster's confessions, the charges against your mother have been dropped." Jimmy inclined his head toward the parking lot. "Go home. Hopefully, there's some leftovers after all your guests."

After another round of thanks, Kirsten, Mom, and Donny headed out to his car. Kirsten sighed. Funny, how this Thanksgiving could be the best and worst one she ever had.

And none of it involved food.

Chapter 32 

At precisely one o'clock on the last Sunday afternoon of November, Kaley pulled a perfectly roasted small turkey from the Wilson's oven. Penn and Teller perched on the kitchen table, their eyes focused on the bird. Kirsten had given up trying to shoo the two out of the kitchen.

Once Kaley set the pan down on the counter, Kirsten hugged her from behind.

"I'll make the gravy and mash the potatoes," she murmured in Kaley's ear.

She laughed. "Since when do you like kitchen duty?"

"Since you took care of everything, and let me and Mom sleep in this morning." Kirsten grinned.

And her twin had. The two pumpkin pies and the fresh bread sat on cooling racks. Kaley popped the green bean casserole into the oven.

"Well, I could use the break." Kaley pulled off the oven mitts and handed them over to Kirsten before she sauntered into the dining room where River was helping Dad set the table.

"Need some help?" Donny peered around the edge of the refrigerator.

"Sure." Kirsten pointed at the huge pot of cooked, and drained potatoes. "Cut up a stick of butter and add a cup of cream to those and mash 'em."

He took off his coat and hung it up before he washed his hands.

Meanwhile, she dumped the ingredients for the gravy into a saucepan and gently stirred in the cornstarch mixture.

"Robbins is right." Donny cut chunks from the stick of butter and let them drop into the still steaming potatoes. "We make a pretty good team."

"How do you know what he said to me?"

"He told me the same thing as he was leaving." Donny measured the cream and poured it into the pot. "Don't you think we do?"

"Yeah, we did make a good team." She smiled at him.

"Good because Chief Hall and Sheriff Birkheimer offered me a place on the taskforce." After adding salt and pepper, he smashed the potatoes with a certain intensity she never saw before. Nor would he meet her gaze.

"Part of the stipulation is that we take criminal justice classes," she said. "How—"

"I got a scholarship." Pride and embarrassment warred within him from the sharp spikes in his aura. "From the Dare Coven." He paused in pounding the potato mixture and eyed her. "And I know you got one from Brown Dog."

Her face heated. "Yeah, but it's specifically for Ashland."

"I'm not sure I want to do college. I think you were right when you told Ellie that school wasn't necessarily right for everyone." He poured a bit more cream into the mashed potatoes before he added, "What would you think if I went to the law enforcement academy after high school and joined the taskforce as their so-called adult member?"

She paused in stirring the gravy. "Are you sure that's what you want?"

"Yeah." He smiled at her. It wasn't his usual cocky grin though, and for some weird reason she liked that smile.

Mom charged into the kitchen. "Why didn't you girls wake me up—" She paused and looked at Kirsten and Donny. "Didn't mean to interrupt you two." She darted towards the dining room and started ordering Dad, River, and Kaley around.

"Did she interrupt something?"

"Just this." Donny kissed her.

And for a first kiss, it was pretty darn good.

Turn the page for a sneak peek at *Feline Navidad!*

Bonus Excerpt, ©2024, Suzan Harden

Feline Navidad

Anxiety jittered along Teller's nerves as he stalked into Penn's room. His brother sprawled on the bed he shared with his human Kaley. In other words, Penn's usual spot when he wasn't demanding their humans serve him extra portions. Teller leapt onto the mattress and rubbed his cheek against Penn's golden cheek.

Only to receive a swat.

At least, Penn hadn't used his claws.

"The girls aren't home yet," Teller said.

"You woke me up to tell me an obvious fact?" Penn yawned and stretched.

"Winter Break starts today. They should be home by now." Teller jumped onto the nightstand and stared out the window. The leaves had long since fallen from the ancient maple tree in the front yard. Gray clouds masked the sun. The asphalt pavement shone from the mix of rain and sleet. No human vehicles had rolled up or down the street for quite a while. A faint chill penetrated the glass and made his breath fog on the pane. Only dogs were stupid enough to go outside on days like this. Even cats without a human were smart enough to find a cozy spot and sleep the dreary afternoon away.

"Technically, it starts tomorrow." Penn joined Teller on the nightstand. "You're impatient for them to set up the new tree course."

"Well, it was courteous for Ellie and River to deliver it after the two-shape failed to help our humans bring one home this year."

"Are you still moping about the him? You've always tolerated him before."

"That was before he started sniffing around my human."

"Maybe Kirsten likes slumming it with a canine."

For that remark, Teller knocked his brother off the wooden surface. Penn shrieked and landed with a thump on the rug.

"You jerk!" But rather than attacking, Penn licked the golden fur of his sides and paws back into place. He took fastidiousness to a new level.

"At least, my human picked a two-shape," Teller spat. "Yours doesn't have the sense to stay away from the halfling."

"The sidhe are the reason the two-shapes exist," Penn shot back.

Teller returned to watching for their humans. "All I'm saying is Kirsten could have picked a feline two-shape."

"And where was she going to find one?" Penn didn't bother rejoining Teller on the nightstand. "There are no prides nearby for her to choose from."

Teller's ears flicked. The familiar hum of the girls' specific metal and plastic vehicle had turned onto the asphalt that ran in front of their house. He leapt down from the nightstand and padded out of his brother's room.

He reached the rug at the bottom of the staircase when Penn yowled, "Banzai!"

Teller was already rolling, anticipating his brother's pounce. They swatted each other until the hinges on the back door squeaked.

Teller smoothly rose to his paws. "Are we done?"

Penn glared at him. "Don't knock me off a perch again."

Teller sniffed before he turned, stalked through the living room, and into the kitchen. Penn trotted behind him. The delicious scent of breakfast bacon still lingered in the air from this morning.

"There you two are," Kaley said cheerfully as she hung her coat. "That must have been one serious nap you were taking."

"Penn was," Teller said. "Not me." He passed his brother's human and approached his own. "You're late."

"Hey, sweet'ums." Kirsten lifted him into her arms and kissed the top of his head. Unfortunately, she reeked of the two-form who courted her.

He sneezed.

"You're not getting sick, are you?" She cradled him and scratched his favorite place on his neck.

"Just allergies to your possible mate." However, he was getting the attention he'd been craving since the last full moon. A purr rumbled through his chest.

"Hey, Kirsten?" her sister called. Penn sat next to his human at the entrance to the living room, snickering. "Come see this!"

Teller's human stopped scratching his neck and joined her sibling. "What the—?"

The annual dead evergreen stood in its red bowl of water in front of the huge front window facing the street. No ornaments or lights hung from it yet. But once the humans decorated it, the annual climbing competition between him and Penn would commence.

"Where did that come from? I thought Mom and Dad agreed not to have a tree this year," Kirsten muttered. "Not that they asked us."

"Well, I sure wasn't going back out to the Slaughter's tree farm," Kaley said as she stared at the white pine. "Goddess. I'm still having nightmares about tripping over Warren Simon's body."

"Wonder what changed their mind?" Kirsten asked.

"They didn't," Teller said.

Kirsten ignored him per usual and set him on the living room rug before she pulled her phone out of her pocket. She frowned when her mother's artificial voice started talking.

"Hey, mom! Glad you and Dad changed your minds about getting a tree for the holidays. We'll have both dinner and the box of decorations ready by the time you and Dad get home." She touched the glass on her phone and shoved it back in her pocket.

"Ellie and River really should have told our humans their plan before they set up this annual sacrifice," Teller said. "I can't believe you told the halfling where the water bowl for dead trees was."

"He asked politely." Penn twitched his tail. "And he smells so nice."

Teller growled low in his throat. "Should Kaley allow him to court her, you will not be part of it."

Penn sniffed. "Doctor Ethan thinks so."

"He doesn't know you are fawning over River because he smells like catnip to you," Teller shot back. "And the fool is accidentally emitting the odor in order to make you like him."

"Or maybe he's doing it on purpose to please me," Penn mocked.

"He's not that bright."

"You're confusing the two-form's lack of intelligence with River's natural brilliance."

"Brilliance, my fluffy tail," Teller muttered.

Kirsten's phone rang. "Hey, Mom."

Rachel Wilson shrieked a number of rude invectives before she said, "I did not bring any pine tree home."

"But Yule is tomorrow," Kirsten said.

"Get out of the house! Now!" Rachel demanded.

"Did she really just say that?" Kaley rolled her eyes.

"It's a gift," Teller said. As usual, the twins ignored him. His human could barely communicate with him in the best of times. Now, her dam was getting her riled to the point he couldn't get through to her.

"Mom, if you didn't put up the tree, maybe Dad did," Kirsten said.

"Get the cats, get in the car, and come over to my office," Rachel demanded.

"Fine, Mom, but we're stopping at Jo's to get coffee and a snack first," Kirsten replied. "See you in a bit."

Kaley knelt next to the tree and extended her palms. Penn hoped up on her shoulder to observe.

Energy whispered along Teller's fur, even the fine hairs around his nose, and he sneezed again.

Kirsten picked him up again. "Maybe we should take you in to see Dad. I know you got your flu vaccine, but I don't want you sick for tomorrow."

"Yeah, he's sick in the head," Penn muttered.

"I agree, Snookums." Kaley carefully got to her feet so she wouldn't dislodge Penn. "We don't detect any magick in or around the tree."

"Let's swing by Dad's clinic first," Kirsten said. "We can have him check out Teller's sneezing and ask him about the tree."

"But we're taking both cats, right?" Kaley asked.

"That's what Mom said to do," Kirsten replied with a thick layer of resentment.

Teller wanted to protest, but he knew it wouldn't do any good. The last time he tried, his human's dam had paralyzed him with a spell and shoved him into his carrier anyway.

Can Teller and Penn convince their humans nothing is wrong before they do something drastic to the thoughtful gift? Because everyone knows you don't reject a gift from a fae, even if he's only half-fae.

Check out *Feline Navidad* coming December 1st!

Acknowledgements

First of all, a huge thank you to my cover artist Valerie Lennox and my formatter JW Manus for their work on this book. I couldn't have done it without them.

When I originally wrote this book, we were three months into the COVID-19 pandemic and its resulting lockdowns. Darling Husband and I were wearing masks and gloves everywhere we went.

Frankly, I didn't have a choice about going to doctors' offices. I was still undergoing treatment for breast cancer at the time. However, appointments were often rescheduled when the doctors or their staff contracted COVID-19 despite all of our precautions. Even worse, one of my doctors was pregnant with her first child in the middle of this mess. And then there was my poor father-in-law trapped in his assisted living apartment, his only physical company the gowned, gloved, and masked nurse who brought him his pills.

As I've said in the Acknowledgments in *Spells and Sleuths* and *Fae ad Felonies*, it was not a good time for any of us, and my own fear and anxiety were amply, but unconsciously, demonstrated in the first three books of this series. However, I've learned my lesson. This will be the only time I pull any of my stories from the retail sites because they didn't meet my usual criteria.

Things have gotten better, though I still often wear a medical or N95 mask to the cancer center here in town out of a pound of prevention. Last thing I want to be is a carrier who infects folks whose immune systems are even worse than mine.

But most of all, I'm having fun writing again. And I've having a fang good time writing the next story in the Millersburg Magick Mysteries series. Teller can be as snarky as his witch Kirsten, and I'm getting a kick writing the Christmas story from his perspective.

Happy Holidays from me and my characters to you and your families!

About the Author

SUZAN HARDEN transitioned from writing information technology manuals for companies and legal articles for a law enforcement magazine to her first love, fantasy and science fiction in all their forms. She's the author of the Bloodlines, the 888-555-HERO, and the Justice series.

www.ingramcontent.com/pod-product-compliance
Lightning Source LLC
Chambersburg PA
CBHW011225190726
48287CB00008B/2744